4 $\frac{75}{KWZ}$

A TRAVELLING WOMAN

Books by John Wain

THE CONTENDERS

LIVING IN THE PRESENT

BORN IN CAPTIVITY

PRELIMINARY ESSAYS

A TRAVELLING WOMAN

A Novel

BY

JOHN WAIN

ST MARTIN'S PRESS

New York

ARTHUR'S

I'm not good-looking
And I don't dress fine
But I'm a travelling woman
With a travelling mind.

Traditional, *apud* Bessie Smith

'WELL, as I keep saying,' said Janet Links, 'I think psycho-analysis would help you.'

George Links stared at his wife with his habitual listless moodiness. He was trying to remember why he had married her in the first place. It was only four years ago, but he found he could not remember.

'The name itself is an ignorant coinage,' he remarked in his thin, scholarly voice. 'I'd like to know where they think that "O" comes in. It should really be "psychanalysis" — either that or——'

Janet Links did not wait to hear the rest of the sentence before beginning to shuttle the tea-things about, preparatory to taking them into the scullery for washing. They were sitting in the kitchen of their cottage in a small Oxfordshire country town. It was a pleasant cottage, the town itself was reasonably attractive, and George Links, who at twenty-eight was a junior partner in an old-established firm of country solicitors, could not be said to be doing badly. Nevertheless, he did not feel happy, and made no secret of the fact. It was now autumn, and the previous summer, alleging to himself the boredom of country life as his motive, he had become entangled with the wife of one of his senior partners, a Mrs. Elsie Cropper. His wife, discovering at once what he was doing, had broken up the idyll by threatening to bring it to Mr. Cropper's notice, ignoring George Links's protest that if she did he would be sacked and they would both starve together. They had no children, largely because George Links was unable to see himself in the role of parent, and she preferred the prospect of starvation to the present reality of sharing her husband with Mrs. Cropper, a red-haired woman fifteen years younger than Mr. Cropper and twenty-one months older than George Links.

As it happened, Mrs. Cropper was not really George Links's type, and not even the highest concentration of self-deception could make him think, except for a few minutes at a time, that Janet had robbed him of something valuable by breaking up the *liaison*. What he really needed, and needed quite consciously, was something to grumble about; and he had, over tea, been explaining how much he needed it, while Janet half listened and half merely waited for him to finish, so as to bring up her own invariable suggestion: that he should seek the help of a psycho-analyst.

'. . . to anchor this floating body of resentment to some fixed point outside myself,' George Links had finished, stabbing the air with his teaspoon. He did this as if aware that the teaspoon was silver and dated from the eighteenth century. He had no money to speak of, and neither had any member of his family for several generations back, but the Linkses had faint but unmistakable pretensions to gentility; a few pieces of Georgian silver, a family portrait or two, and the odd item of Sheraton or Chippendale furniture, were jealously husbanded, bequeathed, and shared out among them as important emblems of Links taste, traditional Links discrimination. George's contribution to the family continuum of *bon ton* was his pedantry. He spent some time each day in reading the more stylish newspapers with an eye open for split infinitives, imprecise uses of metaphor, and ignorance-revealing mistakes in spelling, such as 'rhodomontade'. To ferret out such a mistake, and gravely indicate its presence by a deliberate pecking movement of the hand holding a Georgian tea-spoon, could usually be counted on to make his day. He was thin and rather stooping, with sandy hair; except when he was being pedantic, he could not be called bad-looking, in the desiccated way that some men affect until it becomes their nature; but he was being pedantic a good deal of the time.

Janet, too, was not bad-looking, except when she was wearing her glasses, which had large and ornate rims and went up to a point at the corners. They looked like carnival glasses, deliberately assumed as part of a silly disguise. The best feature of her face was her high cheek-bones, and the spectacles ruined the effect of these. George Links, had he ever looked at her closely enough, might have noticed this, but he was given to saying that women resented any interference by their menfolk in the all-important mysteries of dress and appearance. In the first months of their marriage Janet had sometimes asked him, 'How do I look?' and he had broken her of the habit by answering each time, 'You must know already that you look all right, or else you wouldn't bring your appearance to my attention.'

So, this Sunday afternoon in November, he had

ridden the hobby-horse of his dissatisfaction up and down the length of Janet's patience, which was considerable; leaving her, as she cleared the tea-things away, to make her usual exit-line.

'I think psycho-analysis would help you.'

She was already moving away into the kitchen, certain in advance that George Links would receive the suggestion with a moody silence. But this afternoon was the memorable one, the point where it all began. For her husband, speaking with theatrical quietness, pulled her up short half-way to the scullery door with: 'You may very well be right.'

Janet kept very still, with her weight distributed equally on both feet. To move might be to spoil everything.

'I might very well be what?'

'Right.'

She moved a few more paces, disappeared through the scullery door, and could be heard setting the dishes down on the table before she came back and confronted him.

'George.'

'Yes.'

'You say I'm right? You *do* think an analyst could help you?'

'I think a psychanalyst could help me.'

Impulsively she knelt by his chair, so that their faces were level.

'Darling — and you'll find one and go to him?'

'I *have* found one.'

She seemed ready to faint with delight, as if he had won a football pool without telling her and now revealed that he had spent the money on a mink coat, a Rolls-Royce and a staff of household servants who were at that moment waiting outside the back door, ready to enter and begin work immediately by washing the tea-things.

'You've *found* one? Already . . .? But who——'

'Captax put me on to one.'

For an instant she looked troubled; Fredric Captax was an old friend of George Links's whom she had never met, and for this quite sufficient reason she distrusted him.

'Are you sure Captax is reliable? It's so important to get a good——'

'Captax is a medical man. He has a wide acquaintance among doctors of all kinds.'

'Including abortionists.' (This was true, and George Links had once been unwise enough to pass on to his wife an anecdote about Captax and an abortionist friend of his.)

Aware of having missed a trick, George Links said stiffly, 'To be sure. Doctors and medical men of all kinds. Some of them are abortionists. Others specialise in removing portions of people's spinal vertebrae and replacing them with ball-bearings made of plastic. Others again spend their time giving nervous breakdowns to dogs by setting them tasks beyond their comprehension. There's probably no category of doctors in which he hasn't got a few acquaintances. So when I happened to mention to him that you thought I should consult a psychotherapist, he immediately——'

'Oh, darling! Did you *really*?'

'. . . And now I've told you, I'm going to go ahead and make an appointment for a preliminary——'

5

'Oh, George, *darling* . . . Will you *really*?'
'A man named Volumis.'

.　　.　　.　　.　　.

George Links was, in all this, blamelessly telling the truth. He had genuinely consulted Captax, over lunch on his last visit to London. Captax was not strictly a doctor; he was a research worker in pathology, with a reputation for competence which gave him the *entrée* to most quarters of the medical world. George Links's story departed from the truth by falling short of, rather than overshooting, the limits of complete frankness.

'And now, damn it,' he had said to Captax petulantly, as they ate *scampi*, 'she's taken it into her head that I'm not good enough as I stand: she wants to have me altered.'

'Altered?'

'Messed about with mentally. Wants me to have psycho-analysis.'

Captax looked thoughtful for a moment, fingering a piece of toast. A pyknic type, with a potato-face and domed forehead, he easily looked thoughtful. Then, a gleam in his deep-set eyes, he looked up.

'And of course you're going to do it.'

'Of course I'm *not* going to do it. As if I hadn't got enough to bother about . . . it's nothing short of——'

'*Don't be an ass.*'

George Links fell silent, and Captax, after repeating solemnly, 'Don't be an ass,' went on, prodding the air above his plate with a blunt finger:

'There aren't any psycho-analysts in the country,

6

where you live. So you'll have to come up to town, and
fairly frequently too. Advantage number one: frequent
visits to town on your Tod Sloan — no need to account
for your doings. Leave her to keep the home fires
burning.'

'Yes, that's all very well, but I——'

'Just what all you married men are always scheming
and plotting to engineer — and here it is dumped in
your lap. Advantage number two: it goes on for
years. You'll have time to settle in to all your old
routines — become a familiar figure again in the old
spots.'

'Sounds all right in theory, but I don't know when
you expect me to fit it all in. I'll be dashing for trains
half the time.'

Beaming, Captax stabbed the air even more vigorously. 'Advantage number *three*! To do any good,
you'll have to see the man several times a week. And
so as not to break the current, it would obviously be
best for you to stay at least one night in town.'

At the prospect of several years of licensed overnight
visits to London, George Links began to brighten.
Turning with renewed appetite to his *scampi*, he looked
up only to say, eagerly, 'You're right, Fredric. Fix
it for me, will you? Find me a cheap one.'

.   .   .   .   .

Affably, then, the November sun shone on George
Links as he stepped out of the cottage door one afternoon a week or so after the conversation with his wife.
Wrapped in an agreeable stillness, with the brown
leaves curled and comfortable on their twigs as if no
end-of-the-year gale would ever come to tear them

down, the countryside seemed a stage set, gay and warmly lit, through which he might dance, to the music of a hidden orchestra, towards the yellow brick tower of the railway station. Something of the affability of the sun got into the kiss he gave his wife, the wave he gave her, with his free hand, from the corner of the road, and the spring of his step on the dry ground; something of it stayed with him in the drumming and puffing of the train, in the controlled clamour and suppressed excitement of Paddington Station, in the smooth, patient stopping and starting of the bus — and the last drops of it had scarcely evaporated when he found himself on the doorstep of a house in a quiet street, staring, with gathering anxiety, at the plain metal plate: 'Mr. C. Volumis.'

★ II ★

THE saloon bar was very full, and at first George Links did not see Captax, who was in a corner with his back to the room, talking to a very pretty girl and a fair-haired, willowy young man. But by the time he had bought himself a drink and raised it to his lips, Captax had turned, seen him, and was beckoning.

'Well, how did it go?' he asked in a jovial, half-rallying tone.

'All right,' said George Links non-committally; he was not eager to begin discussing his analysis, a topic on which he felt sensitive, in front of strangers.

'Just preliminaries this time, I expect,' Captax went on, nodding his head.

'Introduce me.'

'Well, it's a long way round to get to a simple point, but it ought to——'

'Introduce me.'

The girl laughed across at George Links — rather invitingly, he thought — and, without waiting for Captax, mentioned her name and that of her husband. George Links nodded stiffly; he was annoyed that the willowy youth should be married to the girl. But he tucked her name away in his memory: *Barbara Bone.* He surmised that her maiden name had been some-

9

thing more elegant than Bone; something, at any rate, that did not alliterate with 'Barbara'.

'George has been seeing his analyst,' said Captax grandly, as if proud to be associated with a man who had an analyst.

'Really, have you?' said Barbara Bone, leaning forward slightly. 'Does he do you good? Do you go often? Very often, I suppose. Does he make you do free association? I expect you lie on a couch, don't you?'

'Yes.'

'What d'you mean, yes?'

'Yes I have and he does do me good and I do go often and I do go very often and he does make me do free association and I do lie on a couch.' George Links smiled as he reached the end of his sentence, to blunt any possibly wounding effect. He was aiming at a tone of light badinage, not discouraging sarcasm.

Barbara Bone's husband said, 'A head-shrinker. Your head doesn't look as if it's shrunk.'

'How long have you been going to him?' asked Barbara Bone.

George Links felt unwilling to admit, after all this, that he had only just been for the first time and had not even lain on the couch yet. So he said, 'Oh, ages. It's a long business, you know.'

Captax had been over at the bar, asking for cigarettes, during this exchange; he now came back and said, 'Well, the next thing we must do for George, having found him an analyst, is to fix him up with some digs. Then he can really get started.'

Barbara Bone's pretty, oval little face looked from one to the other, puzzled.

'Get started? I thought——'

'He's just kicked off this evening, haven't you, George?'

'Yes,' said George Links between his teeth.

'But you said——' Mrs. Bone began. Then she broke off, shot a sympathetic look at George Links, and, probably to cover up the awkward moment, bent her head and began to rummage in her handbag. Obviously she now thought of him as a mental cripple, a pathological liar who was doing the only possible thing, for the sake of himself and society, by seeking psychoanalytical treatment.

George Links looked coldly at Captax, who merely said, 'We'd better start thinking at once. Where does the man hang out, George? Has he got a consulting-room, or d'you go to his house?'

'I go to his house. It's near Swiss Cottage.'

'Swiss Cottage, eh?' said Captax musingly. 'Now who do we know who lives that way? Can't you two think of anybody who might find George a corner to sleep in, once a week?'

Barbara Bone's husband put his glass down carefully, evidently so as not to spill his drink, and then began writhing and jerking with laughter.

'What is it, Evan?' she asked him.

Evan! George Links thought.

'You know what it is,' he said, between curiously well-controlled gusts of laughter. 'You know who lives out there.'

'You mean——'

'Of course!' shouted Captax, beginning to dance up and down. '*Ruth!*'

'But yes!'

'Just exactly what he's——'

'RUTH!'

They all laughed for a long time. George Links did his best, meanwhile, to conceal the pain he was feeling. Some fundamental insecurity in his nature made it particularly abhorrent to him to feel left out. He stood quite still, holding his glass in his rigid right hand, waiting for them to let him in on their laughter as tensely as one waits for the dentist to stop drilling.

Instead of entering on any explanation, however, Captax, once the first frenzy of his laughter had spent itself, simply grabbed George Links by the elbow and said, 'This way. Quick now — no time to waste.'

'Where are we going?'

'To the telephone, of course.'

They went down some steps. The instrument awaited them. Captax began to search his pockets for pennies.

'What exactly are you up to, Fredric?'

'You'll see. Right, that's three. I want one more. Come on, surely you've——'

'Yes, yes, I dare say I've got a penny, but first I want to have some idea of——'

'Ah, here's one. Right, I shan't need yours.' George Links noticed that Captax dialled the number from memory. 'Hullo, is that you, Ruth? Yes, Fredric. Fine, thanks. Listen, Ruth, get ready to be asked a favour. Are you ready? I'll tell you what kind. No, don't be alarmed. It's simply that there's this fellow, this friend of mine, George Links his name is, who needs a room one night a week in your district. Yes, only one. It's his analyst. His analyst lives there. Well, look, I thought it wouldn't be too difficult for you to . . .'

A week later, George Links, carrying a small suit-
case, walked down the calm tree-lined street looking
at the numbers, found the right one, unlatched the
gate, walked up to the door and rang. While waiting
for an answer he looked round the garden; it bore
witness to a love of growing plants which extended to
many types commonly regarded as weeds. Whoever
tended it had scattered mixed flower-seeds lavishly and
allowed the results, if any, to compete as best they
could with the hardier sowings of nature and chance.
Nature and chance, at the present moment, were
making the better showing.

He rang again. The afternoon quiet was more
intense than it would have been in his own village.
Were they out? But this Ruth had told Captax,
telephoning from the pub, that she would be in to
receive him and to discuss the terms on which he might
rent an attic room in her house for one night a week.
He rang again.

A tall man in a dark-blue jersey and flannel trousers
came round the side of the house. He was large-
limbed and walked as if put together rather loosely,
with plenty of play at the joints.

'I thought I heard the bell,' he said. 'I was in the
garden. Would you be Mr. Links?'

'Yes.'

'I'm Edward Cowley.'

He seemed to bring out the name with a slight,
barely perceptible effort, as a man does who knows
that his name will be familiar to the person he is
addressing. It was as if he knew that the four syllables
'Edward Cowley' were more than a combination of
sounds by which he identified himself — were, in fact,

charged with a significance that made it, in however tiny a way, a decisive action to utter them.

George Links, who had realised before hearing the name that this must be Edward Cowley, spoke his own two syllables and took Cowley's outstretched hand momentarily in his own. It was a strong, dry hand, though smooth-skinned, as if the labour that had strengthened it was a distant memory. He accepted Cowley's invitation to follow him into the garden, and they moved off.

Rounding the house, they entered a quiet, walled garden which repeated, on a larger scale, the *motif* of profusion already stated by the smaller plot at the front. On the brick path, full in the rays of the bright autumn sun, was an upturned box.

'I was sitting on that,' said Edward Cowley, as if anxious to make the position clear before beginning some complicated bout of negotiation, 'but I'll go into the house and get a chair for you.'

'Oh, don't bother,' said George Links mechanically. 'Another box will do.'

'But a chair would be so much better,' Cowley said in a voice that half coaxed, half pleaded. 'A light cane chair that wouldn't be heavy to carry out . . . you'll see. . . .'

As if afraid that George Links would change his mind, he opened a door whose upper half was of patterned glass, and disappeared into the house.

Left alone, George Links reflected on the nature of his sensations on meeting the bearer of a name he had so long known. Edward Cowley, author of *The Discovery of Faith*; 'a book that has brought the realities of the Christian religion home to thousands of hearts,' as some widely-quoted pundit had said. For years George Links had seen copies of the book everywhere; in one or another of its many editions, in various shapes, sizes, colours and weights, it had stared at him from library shelves, bedside tables, railway bookstalls, and peeped out from the pockets of strangers walking past in the street, from women's shopping bags, from the heaped-up jumble of second-hand barrows. *The Discovery of Faith*. A book he had not read, a book he had never for a moment considered reading, and yet a book without which the religious revival of the 'forties, and its steady continuance into the 'fifties, would have been scarcely imaginable. Edward Cowley's large, expressionless face, with its thinning, tousled hair, strong nose and chin, and wide mouth, had been for years as familiar to George Links as his own. It never varied, whether encountered in large scale as part of the display in a bookseller's window, or in small scale on the back of some varnished paper-covered edition of *The Discovery of Faith*; presumably Cowley had once in his life been driven under a photographer's arc-lamps, and was willing for that one experience to be his last.

The royalties! George Links thought to himself. The hundreds of thousands of copies, the translation rights, the magazine extracts, the radio adaptations! Yet they did not seem to live very well. Cowley must be able to afford a better house than this, but he and Ruth chose to live here, conspicuously below their income. *Ruth!* When was he going to see her?

Cowley reappeared, carrying a cane armchair, and George Links controlled the wave of curiosity and impatience that surged through his mind. At all costs none of it must appear in his face: he was quite frank with himself as to the nature of his curiosity about Ruth, and it was not a kind her husband should be allowed to guess at.

Gravely, registering nothing except punctilious gratitude, he thanked Cowley for the chair, settled himself in it, and watched Cowley resume his seat on the box.

There was a lull. For a moment they sat looking at each other; George Links allowed the ideas of Cowley's royalties and wife to spin rapidly through his mind; both unknown quantities, and both attractive themes for speculation.

Cowley sat quite still, his hands on his knees, his head slightly inclined in an attitude of formal meditation. He seemed to be considering how best to begin a conversation, and on what theme. After a time he raised his eyes and said, 'Ruth should be back by about six.'

'Yes?'

To gain time for a further study of Cowley, George Links took out his cigarette-case.

'Cigarette?'

Cowley shook his head. 'Thanks, I don't smoke.'

Of course you don't, George Links thought. Lighting a cigarette himself, he eyed Cowley through the smoke. How could he have thought that this monolith of a man could have any nervous habits? — or any left-over flickers of energy that he had to find a way of using up? As Cowley sat there on the box, utterly still, he gave the impression of a man who had managed to turn all his energies inwards, to set them flowing endlessly into a centre. A centre of what? Meditation or suffering? Calm or tumult? It was not clear, at this stage; perhaps it never would be. But the effect of this enigma was to set George Links's curiosity still more on edge. If this was the husband, why should not the wife be even more remarkable?

The still sunlight lay quietly on the garden; it seemed to ring Cowley's face with a hard, metallic aureole, and suddenly George Links found the lines beating in his head—

> *O sages standing in God's holy fire*
> *As in the gold mosaic of a wall . . .*

That was it exactly; it put into words the effect Cowley had on him. The man was a sage, half-way to being an actual saint. With his large, smooth face, quietly holding aloof from any trace of expression, he looked like some westernised version of the Buddha. His long, powerful body, disciplined to remain absolutely still on its uncomfortable perch, reinforced the impression. And he had offered this figure a cigarette!

'I expect you know what I —— ' George Links began suddenly, full of a nervous impulse to talk about some fairly neutral matter. 'That is, you probably know this man Captax——'

'Only slightly, as a matter of fact. It's really Ruth who knows him.'

'Ruth knows him, does she?' It was a woman's voice, pitched so as to cut dramatically across theirs. 'How nice to come back and find oneself being talked about. But tell me, who is this I know?'

⋆ III ⋆

*T*HIS *is Ruth*, George Links kept saying to himself
as he got to his feet, and the thought seemed
the most important one he had ever had.

'You must be Mr. Links. How d'you do?'

'How d'you do?' (*This is Ruth. This is Ruth.*)

Snippets of conversation with husband. Did you
have a nice tea-party, etc.? Yes, etc. Did the man come
while I was out to mend the, etc.? Yes (no), etc. And
George Links standing rooted there, sunk in concrete,
trying not to stare. *This is Ruth.*

His eyes rested on her in short, furtive spasms
of observation. By directing each glance cannily
to a pre-selected objective, he was able to take
in and store up the details of her appearance without recourse to noticeable staring. In between, he
let his eyes travel over the garden, up to roof-level,
into the branches of trees, down to the earth at his
feet.

One stabbing glance at her face, and away. Another
at her neck and shoulders, and away. She moved so
as to present the back of her head to him for a
moment; the next glance was at her hair-style.
(Short, dark brown, natural-looking curls.) She was
turning; glance away again. She was presenting

herself to him full-face, speaking to him; the rules allowed him one searching glance straight into her eyes.

George Links glanced — then blinked, startled. For a second, as he gazed into Ruth Cowley's eyes, George Links suffered a distinct hallucination. His physical vision was blurred, was interrupted, was definitely *replaced*, just for that second, by a sudden clarity of mental vision. Instead of Mrs. Cowley's hazel eyes, he saw the eyes of his wife, Janet, brown and serious behind her glasses with their ridiculous, up-swept frames, those frames that ruined the effect of her high cheek-bones. And as he saw Janet's eyes, his heart staggered briefly, as if struck a glancing blow with a mallet.

And yet, damn it all . . .! It wasn't as if he was doing Janet any *harm* by . . .!

And whose idea had it been, anyway, for him to come and see this fool psychologist? Wasting time and money!

Ruth Cowley was speaking to him. Janet's eyes vanished; his heart stopped staggering and began to run forward, with great, bounding steps.

'*I understand you want . . . well, yes, that was the idea . . . it's only an attic, really . . . quite good enough for me, I assure you . . . welcome to it . . . very kind of you . . . oh, please don't think of . . . but I must — enough to cover the wear and tear, and laundering . . . well, if you really want to . . .*'

Then she was leading him upstairs to show him the room he was to occupy one night in the week. It was small, with just room for the bed and one chair, and the steep ceiling proclaimed it, as she had said, an

attic. She drew back to let him go in; he peered round
the door, and in an instant had settled there, annihilated
all the rest of his world, and become The Man in the
Attic, his whole life lived in the ascending waves of
her presence, and the descending waves of his awareness
of her.

'Will it suit you?'

'Supremely.'

. . . . .

Outside in the street the autumnal dusk was sift-
ing down through a blue and orange sky. George
Links shut the Cowleys' gate behind him and walked
purposefully until he had put the length of the
street behind him and turned a corner. Then, setting his bag down with exaggerated care, he leaned
his back against a wall and stood still for a long
time.

Where was it to come from, the resilience to fight
off the emotions that were swarming round him like a
flock of maddened bats?

He knew the answer to that one. Previous experiences
(though no previous experience had been on *this*
scale) had pointed the way. Sanity would be regained
by only one route: that of definition, precision, step-by-
step formulation. What exactly was the impression she
had made on him?

Still leaning against the wall, he applied himself
sternly to the task. In the first place, it was an impression made up of contrasts. She contrived — but
'contrived', even as he formulated it, he knew to be the
wrong word, since the dominant impression, knitting
all the rest together, was one of unforced naturalness —

to suggest all the qualities that make up human personality, and to suggest them at their highest possible concentration.

No good, he thought. *That* didn't pin her down. It was too generalized, too abstract. Bring the legal mind to bear on this. Work through *detail*, albeit detail related to general principles.

Colouring: dark. Hair, not black but deep brown. Probably of a softer texture than black hair. Skin pale. Physical type: light but strong; compact. In another ten years she would probably begin to spread noticeably. But she would never develop into the dumpy, thick-legged type. Overall description of figure: rich, but without approaching the caricature of opulence dreamed of by adolescents. Height: about five feet four inches.

George Links began to feel slightly better. It was wonderful what a difference it made when you got the thing wrapped up in phrases. It seemed to tap the pent-up gases in his chest and let them out with a long hiss of gratitude. *Go on*, he encouraged himself, as the blue dusk gathered round him.

Movements:

He tried to find a phrase for the way Ruth walked, held herself, stood, sat. It was impossible. Why was it impossible?

Because — now he had it — the impression made by her physical movements was part of a more complex overall impression. To measure it, to say that with each step she moved each hip exactly so many centimetres backward or forward from an imaginary line bisecting her pelvis, would be utterly meaningless unless one went further and tried to grasp, in words, what *made* her move as she did; what made her do everything the way she did it.

Back, then, to the starting-point: the blend of contrasts. Put it this way:

Features: a blend of firmness with receptive delicacy. The pale, oval face, the pensive eyes lit by what seemed the glow from a hidden fire, the chin that was strongly delineated and at the same time fine-boned and intellectual. Add them up and what was the total? It was an incomplete total, because it left out her mouth. But George Links was satisfied to have it that way. He wanted to leave her mouth out of consideration for the time being; to bracket it off, so to speak. Step by step, in a matter of such complexity and hair's-breadth equilibrium, was the only possible method.

Total impression of features without counting mouth: firmness plus delicacy. Strength of moulding plus delicacy of chiselling. Qualities: alertness, intelligence, passion. But all *diffused*. There was no monstrously lofty brow to proclaim intelligence, no wild blaze in the eyes to signal passion. These qualities were spread, distributed, portioned out evenly. The strong shape of the upper part of the face, its cheek-bones more accurately describable as 'large' than 'prominent', making the eyes seem deeper-set than they actually were, spoke of passion as well as judgment, of the possibility of surrender as clearly as the habit of control. The delicate lines of the lower half seemed eloquent of sensibility and perception; one would have said that the alertness resided there as much as in the eyes; but at the same time the judgment, the control, the strength, were there.

Plus. *Now go ahead — you've nearly got it.* Find the right words for her mouth, and you're there.

The right words? But how many would be needed? Well, there was no need to economize. He had time. And the dictionary was full of words.

Try the obvious ones first. Sensitive? Ah, hell, no. Of course it was sensitive, but what did that say? Back to the concrete details again.

Description of mouth:

(a) *Width.* Normal. An imaginary line, bisecting each eyeball, and produced vertically downwards, would just miss each corner. (Note: for this experiment, mouth must be in repose.)

(b) *Moulding.* Not unusually full. Lower lip, in normal fashion, fuller than upper. Top edge of upper lip rather remarkably straight, contributing to the generally fine chiselled effect. Downward edge of lower lip, a perfectly regular curve.

(c) *Peripheral areas, any remarks on.* Very small pools of shadow at corners, resulting from firmness of muscular structure which tends to keep corners well tucked in. Beneath the lower lip, a narrow shelf of slightly thinner shadow, elliptically dispelled, in proportion as it nears the centre, by the clean uprising curve of the chin. Faint down on upper lip; towards the centre, imperceptible to naked eye, but at the outward extremities quite clearly visible.

Overall impression of mouth: Sensuality. No, that was wrong, clear it away. Envisage the mouth again, with the mind a verbal blank, and let a descriptive word into the blank—

Sensuality.

No, no, God damn it. Ruth's mouth was not what a casual observer would call 'sensual'. It was as intelligent, as firm, as passionate, as delicate as the rest of her features. It was—

Sensual.

'All right, I give up,' George Links said aloud. He picked up his bag. It was quite dark by now, and the street lamps were shining dramatically.

'Sensual! Hah!' he said, bitterly, and walked on, his shadow flaring darkly in the mist.

.   .   .   .   .

'I really don't know what I'll do with them, Mr. Cropper,' said Janet Links, looking down at the huge bunch of hot-house flowers she was holding.

'My dear Mrs. Links,' Mr. Cropper retorted, his spectacles flashing in his round face, 'what does a woman do with flowers? She strews them about. She uses them to brighten her daily life.'

'Well, it's kind of you to care whether my daily life's bright or not,' she said guardedly.

While Mr. Cropper crowed several times, 'But I do care! I do care!' Janet Links retreated to the other side of the room on the pretext of finding a bowl for the flowers. She was wondering how long she could go on being polite, even as thinly polite as at present, with Mr. Cropper. This was the third time in ten days that he had presented himself on her doorstep with what he never failed to refer to as a 'trifling' gift. She did not see any way of refusing these gifts, and contented herself with waiting, rather numbly, until Mr. Cropper, having chosen his time, should launch the onslaught on her virtue which he obviously had

24

in mind. *Then*, she promised herself, she would let him have it with a vengeance.

Insufferable old idiot!

'And how's George getting on?' Mr. Cropper suddenly asked. As he spoke, he shot her a look full of meaning from behind his thick, round lenses.

'Getting on? How should he be getting on? All right, I suppose.'

'Is that all you've——'

'Well, as far as his health and everything's concerned, I can vouch that he's all right, and as far as his work's concerned, you must know better than I do because you work with him.'

Mr. Cropper looked grave for an instant, even slightly displeased. His bald head, weightily inclined, seemed to reflect the light in a subdued, rather disapproving way. It might have been more becoming, his look seemed to imply, to say 'he works with you,' not 'you work with him'; Mr. Cropper being, after all, the senior partner.

When he spoke, it was to carry this new gravity into their conversation.

'Exactly. George and I work together. That's why I ask, Mrs. Links. Because, of course, when he came and consulted me, as the senior partner, about re-arranging his work so as to allow him a couple of days in town, consulting this — this psychological consultant . . .'

So that was it, bloated Mr. Cropper! You knew George was getting psycho-analysis and so you thought two things, didn't you, obscene Mr. Cropper? First, that our marriage must be on the rocks, because people whose marriages are on the rocks always go to psycho-analysts, don't they, Mr.

Cropper? Second, that I'd be fair game, for one reason and another and being on my own two days a week — eh?

She found two bowls in the cupboard, divided the flowers among them, and put them on the table.

'Excuse me,' she said. 'I must go and get a jug of water.'

'Just a moment before you go,' said Mr. Cropper. He came across the room towards her. 'I just want you to know——' His voice was syrupy with emotion. Nor real emotion, she knew; just the sickly fumes from his belly rising to his head.

'To know what?'

'That you can confide in me.'

'Confide what in you?'

'Just anything, Mrs. Links. You can — you can *depend* on me.'

Over his shoulder, she saw George Links coming up the garden path. It was dark, but the curtains were not drawn and the light shone on him as he approached the window.

'Mr. Cropper, it's nice of you to say I can depend on you, but really I don't see——'

'But you do see, Mrs. Links. Really I'm sure you *do* see.'

She wondered if he knew anything about George's entanglement with his wife. If so, it was doubtless an added spur to his determination. As she wondered, her ears caught the sound of George Links's key in the lock. It was only a slight sound, and Mr. Cropper was too pre-occupied to hear it.

'You need someone, Mrs. Links — Janet — you *need* a man you can turn to. It's a natural——'

'Won't I do?' asked George Links, coming in from

the hall. He was unbuttoning his mackintosh as he spoke, and, coming to a halt in front of Mr. Cropper, he drew it off as if about to fight.

'Aha, George!' Mr. Cropper cried out loudly. 'There you are!'

'Yes, here I am.'

'Got back from town, then?'

'Yes.'

'Back home, eh?' Mr. Cropper's voice rose to a desperate shout, as if sheer loudness would batter the situation into an acceptable shape. 'Had a good trip?'

Janet Links, who could stand it no longer, put in, 'Mr. Cropper was just telling me how glad he was, for your sake, George, that you've found a good psychoanalyst.'

'Telling you——?'

'Yes. He knows all sorts of people who've been very greatly helped by analysis.'

George Links turned to Mr. Cropper. 'That's not what you said the other day.'

Mr. Cropper was on his way out, picking up his hat, winding his scarf round his neck. 'Searched my memory,' he said briefly, over his shoulder. 'Remembered different.'

The front door opened and closed. With a muffled shout of what might have been 'Good-night' or 'Ooh Christ', he was gone.

Husband and wife were left staring at each other across a silent room.

'What was all that?' George Links asked at length.

'He called round to make a pass at me.'

'Well, for God's sake.'

She took one of the bowls of flowers and put it on a small table. 'He brought these, too.'

'He did, did he?'

'Yes.'

With his eyes fixed on her, she went back to the first bowl of flowers and began meaninglessly arranging them.

'George.'

'Yes?'

'Why don't you say something?'

'I'm just trying to get over my astonishment.'

'Is that the chief thing you feel — astonishment?'

'Yes.'

The vase of flowers hurtled across the space between them, turning upside down as it flew, and struck George Links high up on the left shoulder. Water poured down his chest. The vase, which was a metal one, gonged on the floor, and the flowers fell messily at his feet.

'What——'

Then she was clinging to him, her face buried where he could not see it, with only the shaking of her shoulders to tell him that she was crying.

.　　　.　　　.　　　.　　　.

The saloon bar was very full, and at first George Links did not see Captax. Then he found him sitting in a corner reading the sports page of a newspaper.

'Hello,' he said in response to George Links's greeting. 'I'm just studying form. Everyone always says the Pools don't depend on it, and all one has to do is plunge and treat it entirely as a game of chance, but I don't see that. I mean, if you take——'

'Listen, skip that, Fredric,' said George Links impatiently. 'I've got something more important to talk about.'

'Yes,' said Captax, folding up the paper. 'And I expect I can guess what it is, too.'

Captax took a sip from his glass of red wine. Then, taking the stem of the glass between finger and thumb, he revolved it meditatively.

'Ruth?' he asked.

'Ruth, of course,' said George Links, relieved to find the subject broached with no preliminary explanation.

'You've met Ruth and now your one thought is how to get her into bed.'

George Links restrained the gesture of impatience he felt like making. 'I think I've got it worse than that. I think I'd be satisfied just to be within her orbit, without necessarily doing anything.'

'Of course you would — for a time. It's a preliminary phase everyone goes through, if they find the woman attractive enough.'

George Links studied Captax through narrowed lids. 'God, if you knew how I hate you, Fredric, when you talk in that strain.'

'I do know.'

'Then why d'you do it? Don't you mind being hated?'

'Not in the least.'

George Links went over to the bar and got himself a drink. After a moment's hesitation, he also bought a fresh glass of red wine for Captax.

'Coals of fire,' he said, putting it down.

'I suppose you've some motive for heaping them.'

'Of course I've a motive. I'm longing to talk about Ruth, and you're about the only person I can do that with. Firstly because you know her, and secondly because——' He faltered.

'Secondly,' said Captax smoothly, 'because you think of me as an immoralist who won't despise you for running after another man's wife when you've got a nice little wife of your own at home.'

'Not exactly. It would be more accurate to say that I don't care whether you despise me or not.'

'Same thing, George.'

They drank, silently, each feeling the nature of their relationship as irksome and yet unwilling to risk ending it. They had been like this for years; Captax sometimes compared them with galley-slaves who had grown used to being chained to the same oar. 'We'd be equally lost without the oar and without each other,' he would say.

'Well,' said George Links with a sigh, setting his glass down, 'whether you despise me or not, and whether I care or not, I've still got to talk about Ruth. No, by God, there is something else that has even higher priority. The husband. What do you make of Cowley, Fredric? He has me baffled, absolutely fogged. I can't make him out.'

'Can't make out what precisely?'

'*Anything* about him. I don't say he gives me the creeps exactly, but there's a kind of . . . well, a *numinous* feeling associated with him, isn't there? He lives on a completely different plane from everyone else.'

'Different from Ruth's, for instance?'

'Oh, come, don't bring up really difficult questions

like that. Let me walk before I can run. I don't even understand elementary things about the Cowleys, let alone their spiritual relationship.'

'Well, d'you *want* to understand it — except simply as a means of helping you to seize your opportunities with Ruth?'

'Damn it, Fredric, don't be such a bully. Just because you've got me at a moral disadvantage, it doesn't give you the right to grill me like this. What I mean is, I don't understand even the simplest thing about . . . Well, for instance, why do they live so far below their means?'

Captax looked sage, which meant, in his case, that his eyes retreated back into their hollows and became as tiny as currants. He cupped his chin in one pudgy hand.

'What makes you think they do?'

'Oh, come on, for God's sake — I shall begin to think we're talking about two entirely different couples. I'm talking about the *Cowleys*, man: Ruth Cowley, the woman I'm obsessed with, and Edward Cowley, her famous husband, the author of *The Discovery of Faith*. The income from that book alone must be pretty substantial, even now, and what it must have been for the year or two since it was published . . . He must be *rich*.'

'Know what I think?' said Captax suddenly. 'I don't believe he touches a penny of it.'

'Don't believe he——?'

'Touches a penny of it,' Captax repeated. 'Mark you, I don't know him. I only know Ruth. But I know where they live, and I know a good deal about them, one way and another. D'you know he spends

a lot of his time slaving as a crammer — coaching
louts for scholarships?'

'Never!'

'Yes, he does. And he marks School Certificate
papers for London University.'

'Fredric, you're making it up.'

'Cross my heart,' said Captax. 'My guess is that
his slaving, plus a bit of income that I happen to
know Ruth has, just about keeps them in the state
you find them in.'

The reference to Ruth had deflected George Links's
attention. He stared moodily into his glass for a
moment, then said, 'You know a lot about Ruth, don't
you?'

'Not quite all there is to know, don't worry.'

'Just what does that mean?'

'It means I've never had an affair with her, that's
one thing it means,' returned Captax, staring at him in
a bullying way.

George Links flushed; he was conscious of making a
distinct effort to keep his voice steady as he replied,
'I find no difficulty in believing that. What I want to
do is to ask you one simple question. And I'd like a
straightforward answer, whether it's a tactful one or
not. When you first mentioned Ruth's name to me,
here in this bar, you and those other people — *what
made you burst out laughing?*'

'By Jove, here they are,' said Captax. Half rising
in his seat, he began to move towards the door. There,
just coming in, were Mr. and Mrs. Bone.

'Oh damn that!' said George Links urgently. 'Leave
those two out of it for a minute and answer my question.
It's the least you can——'

'Hello, Fredric!' Barbara Bone was squealing excitedly as she came over, followed by her husband. 'So here you are again,' she said to George Links, coming to a halt in front of their table.

'Yes,' he said grimly.

'Head shrunk yet?' asked the male Bone, none too affably, over his wife's shoulder.

George Links ignored the question, but Captax, getting up from his seat, began to welcome the pair effusively, asking them what they were going to drink, and urging them to sit down while he supplied it.

George Links, left alone with the Bones, sat moodily silent. He was fuming with impatience; besides, he disliked the male Bone, and the presence of the female did not exactly soothe him. She was pretty, but, in his opinion, irritating. Now she came and sat next to him in an artless manner that seemed to him false. He knew he was in for a bout of questioning about his analysis.

'How are you getting on with your man?' she opened, predictably.

'My man?' He stubbornly pretended incomprehension.

'Yes, your psychological man, of course.'

'He thought you meant his valet,' put in her husband, sneering.

'Well, considering it's only a fortnight since you last saw me, you can't expect that I'll have much to report,' said George Links stiffly. 'And you can't expect me to report it to *you* if I had,' his tone implied.

'Don't be so stuffy,' said Barbara Bone. 'It's not a clinical report I want. The subject interests me, that's all.'

33

'Shall I recommend you a few books about it?'

'Stuffy,' she said, giving him a strangely pleased look and moving her head about in a manner that, he supposed, would be called 'bridling'. 'I suppose you just don't want to tell me what happens at your sessions because it's not fit for my ears.'

As a matter of fact, remarkably little had so far happened at George Links's sessions, but he seized the opportunity to release his aggressive emotions.

'That's right, it isn't,' he said, looking her straight in the face. 'But I can tell you a few of the milder things that are wrong with me. For instance, I'm a shoe-fetishist.'

'A what?'

'A shoe-fetishist. I make a fetish of women's shoes. They arouse my sexual emotions.'

'Oh, is that all?' she said, looking disappointed, but George Links noticed, with satisfaction, that her husband's narrow face had taken on an apprehensive expression.

'It's uncontrollable,' he said wildly. 'If I find a woman at all attractive, I'm uncontrollably impelled ——' He bent down suddenly and snatched at her nearest foot under the table. The shoe came off easily, and he took it between his two hands and began gazing at it raptly.

'Look here, steady on,' cried the male Bone. 'Remember I'm here, damn it.'

'Thanks for the offer, but your shoes don't interest me. I didn't say I was a *homosexual* shoe-fetishist.'

'What the hell's going on?' said Captax, who had returned in time to hear the last words. 'What on earth are you doing with the girl's shoe?'

34

'Admiring it,' said George Links in an obsessive monotone, his eyes gleaming. Damn them, if they were going to interrupt his most urgent conversations, he would make them pay for it somehow.

'Look here, don't be a fool,' the husband insisted. 'Give it her back.'

George Links glanced at Barbara Bone. As far as he could tell, she seemed to be feeling simply rather flattered. 'Don't you want the other one?' she asked, bending down as if to slip it off.

Suddenly he felt a surge of irritation at the silly charade he was playing. A squalid farce, played out with no better motive than to annoy a couple whose chief offence was merely that they were present . . . Enough!

He put the shoe down, deliberately, on the table, and said, 'Now you're all here, there's a question I want to ask you. I really wanted to ask it of Fredric on his own, but as you two have happened along you might as well give me *your* answer too.'

'Well, spill it,' said Captax, eyeing Barbara Bone's stockinged foot.

'You remember the last time we were here, when we were discussing the question of finding me a place to stay in once a week. All at once somebody said "Ruth", and then you remember what happened? *You all burst out laughing.*'

Barbara Bone's husband gave a thin, metallic snigger, conveying little apart from a desire to be offensive.

'I want to know why you laughed.'

'Why we laughed?' asked Captax, his face puckered.

'Yes. I've met Ruth Cowley since, and I didn't find anything funny about her.'

Evan Bone, acting, with patent falsity, the part of
a man for whom this last revelation was too much, set
down his glass and gave a high-pitched hoot of laughter.
When the others failed to join in, he intensified the
noise with a kind of desperation, rocking his body to
and fro and repeating:

'He didn't find anything funny about her!'

'*Why did you laugh?*' George Links demanded of
Captax.

Captax looked irritated. 'Seems a pretty unnecessary
question,' he said. 'We laughed because the idea of
sending you round to Ruth's place as a lodger struck
us as funny.'

'Because?'

'Because nothing. You can take it from there
yourself.'

George Links gave each of them in turn a look of
hatred.

'I knew it. Dirty little innuendoes. Innuendi,' he
mechanically corrected himself. 'You're all unwilling
to say anything openly, and so you——'

Evan Bone poked his head forward on its long neck
and said sharply, 'Who's afraid to say anything
openly?'

'You are. You and your wife and Captax.'

'We don't want to be unkind, that's all,' said Barbara
Bone. She seemed disappointed that the conversation
had wandered away from the subject of George Links's
concupiscence towards her shoes.

'I'm not in the least afraid of saying things openly,'
her husband said to George Links.

'All right then, say it.'

'Say what?'

'That she's a whore, damn you!' George Links shouted.

Several patrons looked sharply over at them, but the din of conversation served to prevent his words from carrying across the room and getting them turned out.

Evan Bone seemed flustered by this sudden display of intensity; instead of flaring up in return, he sat back and said sullenly, 'I never inferred she was that.'

'No, you implied it,' said George Links, staring at him coldly. 'Only the hearer infers. The speaker *implies.*'

Captax gave a loud guffaw. 'Isn't that George all over!' he shouted. 'Give him a chance to be pedantic and he'll drop whatever subject he's talking about and——' He finished with another bray of laughter, amid which he first slapped his thigh and then, as if the paroxysm of mirth made him vague about his movements, flung his arm round Barbara Bone's shoulders and drew her towards him in a rough hug. The pretence of absent-minded impetuosity deceived no one; Mrs. Bone reacted by showing signs of a pretty confusion, her husband by flushing darkly and then turning white. It was not, all things considered, his evening.

To cover the embarrassment of the moment, Mrs. Bone turned to George Links and, obviously with the motive of turning the spotlight on him rather than herself, asked, 'Why this sudden concern for Mrs. Cowley's reputation? You seem to make a very personal matter of it.'

Unprepared for the question, and left empty by the ebbing away of his anger of a moment before, George Links had no answer, though he was aware that all three of them were studying him carefully and waiting for him to speak. He hesitated a moment, then swiftly bent under the table and hitched off Mrs. Bone's remaining shoe.

With her agonised giggle tintinnabulating in his ears, he straightened up, placed the shoe precisely on the table alongside its fellow, and, bowing ironically to the company, left the building.

★ IV ★

I MUST *act decisively*, George Links thought, walking up the path through the profusely fertile garden. *I must begin to lay definite siege to her.*

He rang the bell and waited. It was his third visit; so far, he had merely exchanged a few civilities with his hostess and, more rarely, his host. No progress was discernible. His one attempt at an overture, when he had tentatively allowed it to appear that he had the disposal of a certain amount of leisure time in London, had, to all appearances, been ignored.

The door was opening. He composed his face into a smile, warm and boyish, but with the hint of reserve fitting to a member of the Links dynasty.

A boy of about eight, with a large head, pale short hair, and a gnome-like face, stood before him.

'Is it foggy?' the gnome asked.

'Hello! Who are you? What? Is it foggy, you say? No, not at all. Well, just in patches,' said George Links, his composure seriously disturbed by this unexpected addition to the *dramatis personae*.

'There weren't any patches of fog on the up line?' the boy continued, anxiously.

'The up line?'

'I mean, did any of the expresses get held up?'

A trace of impatience had crept into the child's tone.

'Give Mr. Links a chance to hang his coat up, darling,' he heard Ruth Cowley's voice, and at the same instant she appeared, smiling, with a tray in her hands.

'If the expresses from the West get held up, it discerlates the whole system!' the boy cried.

'*Dislocates*, darling, and remember we don't all share your interest in railway matters.' She spoke over her shoulder, going past them into the kitchen.

'Who are you?' George Links asked the boy, point-blank.

'Teddy,' said the boy. 'It doesn't matter if you're interested in railways or not — you live on the Western Region, don't you?'

'Yes, I live on the Western Region.'

'Did you come up on one of the trams?' Teddy asked, following George Links, who was following Ruth, into the kitchen.

'The trams . . .?'

'One of the diesel-electrics.'

'I don't think so. There seemed to be plenty of steam about, as far as I remember.'

'Don't think so!' cried Teddy. He looked at George Links incredulously. 'Don't you *know*?' he demanded.

'Oh, Teddy, darling, *do* get ready for bed,' said Ruth Cowley, laughing. She had turned on the taps and was watching the water run into the sink. 'Mr. Links will tell you all about the trains another time, if you'll just give him a chance to get into the house before you throw questions at him.'

'All right . . . Well, will you tell me the number of engine you come up with, each time?'

'Yes, if you like,' said George Links. 'But isn't it

rather cheating to collect engine numbers that way? I mean, oughtn't you to see them yourself?'

'Coo, yes,' said Teddy witheringly. 'It's not for *collecting*. I just want to look it up and see what type of locomotive they're using. The Western Region's one I haven't got very full coverage on.'

He departed for bed, picking up on his way out a stout volume which he hitched under his arm. A manual of railway administration, George Links surmised.

Ruth Cowley turned to him, smiling. 'I didn't tell you I had a son who was an *aficionado* of railways, did I?'

'You didn't tell me you had a son at all,' he said, trying hard to keep his voice easy and careless.

'No, that's right, I didn't. He was away on a visit to an aunt who lives on the Eastern Region. It turned out that there was so much material to be surveyed that he had to stay ten days. I must say it's a tribute to the thoroughness of my tidying-up that you didn't see any signs of his habitation when you were here before.'

'Perhaps I'm not observant.'

He stood staring bitterly into the flickering and spurting kitchen fire. *Nice going. I've made so little impression on her that she doesn't even mention vitally important facts about herself such as that she's a mother. She's so little aware of me that she doesn't care whether I understand the least thing about her.*

'Have you any other children?' he asked, wheeling round to look at her. She had her back to him, so the wheeling round was not very effective as a gesture, but it helped to express his feelings.

'No,' she said, laughing. 'You've now met all the

inhabitants of the house. There's nothing more to come — no animals, no crazy old relatives, no prisoners chained up in the East Wing.'

No prisoners except me, he thought. *But you're probably right: there's nothing more to come.*

'Would you like a cup of tea, now I've finished the dishes?' Ruth asked, wiping her hands. 'I generally have one about now. If you'll go into the sitting-room I'll bring it in.'

George Links only half heard the words, but the idea filtered through that he must go into the sitting-room, and he shuffled away. Outside the sitting-room door he paused for a moment; probably Edward Cowley was sitting there, silent as a reptile, in the centre of a pool of stillness. George Links felt utterly unnerved by the prospect. All at once he wanted to give the whole thing up. He had a quick mental vision of Janet, sitting at home by herself. What would she be doing? Reading a book, probably, with a tray beside her chair holding a glass of milk and an apple. She never ate properly unless he was there. *Why wasn't he there?* Out in the peace of the countryside, away from the dingy bustle of London and this sordid, degrading pursuit of another man's wife — a pursuit so absurdly ineffectual that she didn't even know he was pursuing her; didn't know he existed, except as someone her good-nature allowed to clutter up her house once a week.

He would go home, and be damned to them. And chuck this damned analysis business, too. Waste of time and money. He'd treat Janet decently simply by wanting to. And he *did* want to. Why, by God, Janet had more character in her little finger than——

He pushed open the sitting-room door and went in. No one was there. The fire was burning brightly; an armchair and sofa were drawn up invitingly before it.

George Links went in and sat squarely in the armchair. Probably Cowley was upstairs, seeing that the boy cleaned his teeth, or said his prayers, or something. The author of *The Discovery of Faith* ought to be a dab hand at hearing people say their prayers. Probably he was reading the kid a chapter of the book to send him to sleep in the right frame of mind.

No doubt he'd be down in a minute. Just as well, in any case, that he was always at home. It made it impossible to start any jiggery-pokery with the woman, and after all there couldn't be any temptation to do something that was *impossible* . . .

Ruth Cowley came in with the tea-tray, put it on the sofa and sat down beside it.

'You do take milk and sugar, Mr. Links?'

'George.'

'You do take milk and sugar, George, if I remember rightly?'

'Yes, please.' So she did remember *something* about him.

Only two cups!

'Is your husband out?'

She sighed. 'Yes, poor Edward, he goes out now and then and spends long evenings cloistered with some dreadful philosophical friend of his.'

He does, does he?

Ruth Cowley's face had taken on a solid, meditative expression. She stared into the fire as if thoughts of a serious nature were beginning to crowd in on her.

'Poor Edward,' she said again. 'He's naturally a philosopher, I mean he sees everything with a philosopher's eyes, and he's always turning over some philosophical question or other in his mind, and going off to discuss it with this friend he has . . . But when I tell him his natural setting is a university, and that he ought to be lecturing in philosophy, he just brushes me aside as if I'd said something too stupid to be argued with.'

'Have you any idea why that is?'

'Yes, he doesn't make any secret of it. He says modern academic philosophers aren't philosophers at all, as he understands it. He's got all sorts of reasons. You should draw him out on the subject some time — I'm sure it would do him good to get a fresh viewpoint on it.'

'I don't think I *have* any views about it.'

'Oh, but you must have some attitude, and the important thing is that it would be a *man's* attitude. I can't help seeing it entirely in human terms, as a woman does. To me, the thing that's clearest is that a university philosophical job would suit Edward, and give him the sort of setting he needs for his working life. I don't care whether modern academic philosophy is this or isn't that. Whereas you, as a man, are bound to have *some* reaction that could be put into the kind of terms men use when they discuss these things . . . Oh,' she finished with a gesture of impatience, 'sometimes I feel that real communication between men and women just isn't possible.'

'Not that kind of communication, perhaps.' George Links heard himself speak before he knew what he was going to say. His pulse was hammering. He had forgotten home, Janet, the rest of the world; all he could think of was the presence of Ruth Cowley and the power that flowed from her. It seemed to crackle towards him in waves, burning his skin, making his hair stand on end, stinging his eyes and nostrils.

'Oh, I know all about that,' she said wearily. Glancing at her, George Links noticed for the first time that she looked tired and strained. 'The kind of communication that *is* possible between men and women — on a level deeper than language, and all that. . . . But don't you sometimes wish it were easier, just the same, for the sexes to reach one another's minds by *talking*? Wouldn't it make life simpler sometimes? Don't you find it, for instance, with your wife?'

My wife! George Links felt as if a hose had been turned on him. *I never said anything about any wife!*

'How d'you know I . . .' he stammered.

'How do I know you're married?' She smiled. 'It's very easy, you know, for a woman to tell a married man.'

'No, I didn't know. How?'

'Well, there are all sorts of indications, depending on the kind of man. Some of them are negative indications, you might say. For instance, I could tell you weren't a bachelor from the fact that you made absolutely no reference to your home, or said anything about your day-to-day routine. A man who lives by himself generally does one of two things when he meets a woman. Usually he brings up the topic of his domestic arrangements at once, so as to rub in how helpless he is and get her to mother him. Or, if he's the type who hates women, he lets slip a few remarks

45

about how well organised he is and how nicely he gets along without one.'

'And you thought that because I didn't . . .?'

'Well, in your case I spotted the marks of the husband who's left his home behind and is out to sniff the air of freedom a bit. That's usually the explanation when a man says nothing at all about his home.'

Without attempting any answer to this, George Links picked up his cup of tea and drank about half of it. He felt he must play for time; she was moving too fast for him, and moving, what was more, in what threatened to be the wrong direction.

Setting his cup down exactly in its place in the saucer, he made himself look up into her face. She was looking at him; not staring, just looking as people do in the course of normal conversation. Suddenly the tension inside him rose in a wave and drowned his habitual caution.

'Well?' he asked, brusquely.

'Well what?'

He scowled. 'You're looking at me as casually as if your last remark had been something like, "It was a fine day to start with but it clouded over towards lunch-time."'

'And how should I be looking at you?'

'That's for you to settle. But at least you needn't go on acting the unconscious. You must know you've thrown the ball into play.'

She looked meditative. 'That's how it seems to you, does it?'

'Yes,' he pressed on harshly, almost brutally. His muscles were spasmodically contracted, making it hard to sit in a natural position. He tried to force himself to relax, but his stomach felt as if a live rabbit were flopping and kicking about in it. He began to speak quickly.

'I might have gone on indefinitely keeping within the limits of drawing-room conversation. But you over-stepped them just now, and that makes them difficult to go back to. So you guessed an important truth about me — that I'm a married man who's out to sniff the air of freedom a bit. Your phrase, not mine. And you might have guessed it and kept the guess to yourself — but you uttered it.'

'With the result,' she said slowly, 'that I threw the ball into play: your phrase, not mine. But what is this game we're supposed to find ourselves playing?'

George Links sat back, closing his eyes; a wave of giddiness was sweeping over him. *Too fast!* sounded in his ears like the cry of a drowning man. He felt utterly helpless. The only thing he could do was to press on faster than ever, as a skilful driver will gamble on accelerating himself out of trouble.

'All right, let's take it absolutely straight,' he said, leaning forward with his hands on his knees. 'There's a customary degree of obliquity in these things, but we seem to have deserted it — and once you desert any of it, you might as well desert it all.'

He stopped in amazement. She was laughing. Not mockingly, or with the effect of covering up other emotions she might otherwise betray. Simply laughing, unaffectedly, from sheer amusement.

Halted in mid-career, George Links felt an acute physical sensation of arrest. He felt the colour spreading hotly across his face.

'Have I said anything . . .' he began stiffly.

Ruth was laughing softly, swaying herself to and fro, and at the sound of his voice she went into a fresh paroxysm. Tears began to brim over her lower lids. Reaching out, she took his wrist and clung on to it: at the touch of her hand he instantly became unaware of everything else.

'You're so funny,' she said at last, drawing her free hand across her eyes. He began silently praying that she would not leave go of his wrist. *'Let's take it absolutely straight!'* she rapped out, staring at him grimly. *'There's a customary degree of obliquity . . .'* but on the word 'obliquity' she melted into laughter again.

She's laughing at the way I talk, his mind blazed. *She finds me ridiculous . . .* but that supple body was still rocking backwards, only just out of his reach — and that soft but strongly moulded hand was still closed on his wrist . . . *So I'm ridiculous, am I? Well, we'll see!*

Trembling violently, he seized her round the waist. As he drew her convulsively towards him, he felt, rather than heard, that she abruptly stopped laughing. Desperately, he strained her to him as if his only object was to still the shivering of his body. But the shivering went on, for what seemed minute after minute, until slowly the realization grew in his mind that she was not moving away, not resisting. Only then did his muscles, one after another, stop their anguished fluttering, and, half fainting with her arms round him, he sank into a deep calm.

The fire burnt on, to the accompaniment of its usual range of noises: the tiny crash of hollowed-out coals setting inwards, the quick spurts of flame, the irregular rustling and ticking. Nothing else stirred.

On their first coming together, Ruth had moved back into the corner of the sofa, where a cushion supported her head. Time had stopped. There was no need to move, to think, or to be anything except a quietly beating heart at the centre of a trance. George Links surrendered his concentric identities like an onion; the false outer one first, then the various half-genuine intermediate ones, and finally the innermost secret one. He existed no longer.

He had no idea how long it was before Ruth moved her head slightly and he knew she was going to speak. An hour? A minute? It scarcely mattered. The pause was over; another hard bundle of reality was about to be tossed into his hands.

'George.'

'Yes, Ruth.'

'Say something.'

He tried to think, but nothing happened.

'Go on, say something.'

'I can't — I can't, honestly.'

'Nor can I. Isn't it awful.'

They were silent for a few minutes; then she tried again.

'Well, at least tell me something.'

'What kind of something?'

'Well, like what you're thinking. You must be thinking something.'

'I'm not,' he said, finding a way of talking now that there was a chance to be precise, to indulge in exact definition. 'I'm really not aware of anything except being close to you. It happened too quickly to leave me with any kind of logical framework to put my thoughts in. But I can tell you what I'd be thinking if I were capable of thinking — if you see what I mean.'

'Yes, I do see. What would you be thinking?'

'I'd be thinking how impossible it is to see the next step ahead of us.'

She stirred impatiently, then was quiet again. He went on:

'I know what you feel like saying — why should there be any step ahead of us? And if there is, why should we think about it? But you know as well as I do that there *will* be a step, in one direction or another; and if there is, we'll just have to think about it, that's all.'

'George.'

'Yes.'

'I want another cup of tea. Get up and pour me one, will you?'

Tea? But that was in another lifetime. 'Isn't it hopelessly stewed and cold?'

'Of course not, silly. It's only five minutes since I poured the first cup out.'

He did not move.

'*Please*, George.'

'No. I won't move. I've no guarantee that if we once get up from this position you'll ever consent to go back to it.'

She sighed. 'Do you want guarantees of *everything* before you take any step?'

'Yes,' he said.

A few seconds went by; then he felt her hand on his forehead, his head was gently turned round to face her, and for an instant their lips met.

Released, he straightened up. The tea-pot was still hot. Everything was as it had been in the old world.

He prepared her a cup as he thought she would like it, measuring and pouring with obsessive carefulness. It was magic, he realized; a strong spell that would make it possible for him to speak to her without cancelling out the kiss.

'Was that my guarantee?' he finally dared to ask, when the cup was in her hands.

She looked up at him over the rim of the cup. 'Yes,' she said gravely. 'That's your guarantee. And as you're so fond of precision, let me be precise about *what* I'm guaranteeing. It's entirely a matter of——'

'No!' he cried sharply. The word was forced out of him so loudly that he sank back into his seat in dismay, afraid that he had been heard all over the house, out in the street, everywhere. But Ruth merely smiled.

'It's all right. It just sounded as if you'd sat on a needle.'

'I had,' he said. 'And for God's sake don't run it into me again. Ruth, it isn't *time* for precision yet.'

'When will it be time?' she said calmly.

'I don't know. I can't see inside your head, to know what kind of ideas you're harbouring.'

'All right,' she said, putting down her teacup and sitting up straight. 'I'll tell you what kind of ideas I'm harbouring. I only know one fact about you, but there are several you ought to know about me and I'll give them to you straight away.'

'Before you start — what's the one you know about me?'

'That you want to make love to me.'

George Links wanted to intervene and fill in some necessary background. *Too fast!* sounded again in his ears. He was shocked by her deliberate, almost

surgical way of singling out one essential fact and expos-
ing it. He hated it, when he was forced to look at it in
its nakedness. In his own mind, it lived happily amid
a close, stuffy cluster of other facts, about home and
Janet and psycho-analysis and Mr. Cropper and the
office and Captax. Dragged out from the cluster,
he felt, it was a horribly embarrassing little fact,
one that did him and itself no credit at all.

'Yes, I saw you blink,' she said. 'But it *is* a fact,
so don't try to duck it. And I'll tell you straight away
that, as it happens, I may have my own motives for
letting you make love to me.'

'Well, there's nothing like being flattering,' he
said bitterly. 'Don't go and let me think it's the result
of my irresistible charm, whatever you do.'

'I won't,' she said, and her voice was as cool as
the glance she gave him. 'I'm not even going to tell
you that I like you particularly. No doubt I'll start
liking you if I let you take me to bed: that's the annoy-
ing thing about being a woman. I mean one's emotions
are geared to physical things in that way. If you're
at all satisfactory as a lover I'll probably even be in love
with you, with part of myself at any rate. But that
doesn't mean to say that I'll like you much, even then.
I may, but I can't say.'

He was at a loss for words; all he could do was to
stare at her sadly and savagely.

'I dare say you're thinking that you don't care
whether I like you or not, as long as you get me into
bed. You'll have gained your point and you'll——'

'No, Ruth, don't talk like that, please,' he broke
in. 'I'm going to try so hard to make you like me that
I'm sure it won't be long before——'

'Oh, for God's sake *don't*. Listen, try to understand this, will you? I said I'd got my own motives why I might let you make love to me. All right, well, you ought to know that liking you isn't one of them. If I *liked* you, I don't suppose I'd even consider getting into that kind of tangle with you. That kind of situation, between people who can't marry, is bound to end with a complete break, sooner or later — and generally sooner. Well, I wouldn't like to have a complete break with you if I liked you. Liked you as a person, that is.'

'Don't you even like me a bit as a person?' he asked, humbly. 'It's terribly flattering to the vanity.'

'Don't worry,' she said, giving him a level, expressionless look. 'Once we get started, I'll take care of your vanity.'

The blood drummed in George Links's ears; he gripped the arms of his chair for an instant, then released them and moved towards her; but he had moved no more than a few inches when the door clicked open. He froze, noting as he did so that neither he nor Ruth was in an unusual or compromising position.

'I just wanted to ask you,' said Teddy, coming round the door and fixing his eyes intently on George Links's face, 'if you could make some enquiries for me about the City Class.'

George Links lay back against the cushions, feeling weak.

'Teddy, you ought to be asleep,' said his mother.

'No, but I was just wondering — I must just ask Mr. Links this,' said the boy. 'You know about the City Class?'

'No, I don't,' said George Links faintly. 'What's it a class in? I mean, is it one you want to go to?'

Teddy smiled soberly. 'It's a class of *engine*. City, 4-4-0. They withdrew them in 1931 and just left one. It was in a museum. But they've brought it out now and they use it for special trips for railway enthusiasts.'

'Oh, Teddy, darling, do go to *bed*.'

'Yes, but, Mum, there's only one in existence, and it's on Mr. Links's region. He could easily find out——'

'All right, Teddy,' said George Links, with a warm smile that was really prompted by his relief at getting away so lightly. 'I'll make enquiries and then when there's a trip hauled by this City locomotive I'll take you on it, shall I?'

'Thank you. I expect Dad'll take me,' said the boy politely. 'But I'd be glad if you could find out about it.'

He said good-night and the door clicked shut behind him. George Links sat still. The moment was killed. And why should the boy have so decisively refused even to consider going on an excursion with him? Didn't he like him, or something?

Well, after all, why should he . . . why should anybody?

★ V ★

'AND then afterwards, when she came down, the whole thing took on a different tone,' George Links said to Captax. They were walking across Hampstead Heath.

'Different, how?'

'In every way. She just left me sitting there for about ten minutes, and when she came back it was just as if we'd known each other for twenty years. I was sitting in the armchair, and instead of coming to me she sank down on the sofa and started talking in a sort of monotone — just went on and on. It was as if she wanted to explain everything to me, without much caring how I took it. I mean she never seemed to look up at me to see how I was reacting or anything.'

'Very strange,' said Captax. 'But then Ruth's a strange girl.' He seemed determined to act up to his rôle as the expert on Ruth, considering each newly revealed facet of her character in the light of his long experience of her ways. Actually, as George Links had already guessed, he had only met her two or three times. 'A strange girl,' he repeated.

'Well, anyway, she just talked on and on. Not about herself, still less about herself and me.'

'What about, then?'

'About her husband. She seems — well, it's hard

55

to put it precisely, but — as if she's wrapped up in him.'

'As wrapped up as a woman can be in her husband, anyway, when she's about to launch into an affair with the lodger.'

'That's just it. With one half of her mind — no, more than half, two-thirds at least — she really doesn't seem to think of anything but him. And with the rest she seems to be drifting.'

'Drifting?'

'Just letting herself float. It's an extraordinary impression she gives. For instance, she doesn't seem particularly aware of me as a person. Half the time, I'm just a sort of undifferentiated presence, like a piece of the furniture, except that I'm a piece that needs a certain kind of attention. Like a wireless, say, that needs to be tuned to different stations and so forth. Or a fire that needs making up now and then.'

'I'm not surprised to hear it,' said Captax, lifting his feet carefully as they negotiated a muddy section of the path. 'You aren't a person at all, in her eyes. You're just the lodger who's opportunely come along to fill a gap in her scheme of things.'

George Links flushed angrily. More than any other human being, Captax had the power of making him angry.

'I suppose just anybody would have the same effect,' he said. 'My personality just doesn't enter into it, as you see the situation.' He waited, hoping against hope for a contradiction.

'Exactly,' said Captax, still threading his way between puddles. 'Here's a woman in a certain situation. Enter a lodger, male. And at once——'

'Bloody good!' George Links shouted, his calm suddenly breaking. 'Bloody good, damn you! I confide the details of this delicate situation to you, and you come up with a coarsely stupid——' He choked. 'A grossly silly bloody diagnosis that I could have got from the — from the conductor of the first bus that came along, if I'd chosen to confide in him instead of you.'

'Pity you didn't, then,' said Captax stiffly. 'He'd have nettled your vanity just as easily, and you'd have been less resentful about it, coming from a stranger.'

'I consulted you, rather than a bus conductor,' said George Links, speaking with venomous precision, 'because I hoped to get a little light shed on the situation by someone who (a) knows Ruth, (b) knows me, and——'

'And (c) knows that the thing that holds you together is your pitiful little vanity,' Captax snarled. 'I'm giving you the situation as I see it——'

'*You* see it! You haven't even let me finish telling you the details yet. All you can do is——'

'Details, details!' Captax began jerking his head about, a sure sign that he was losing patience. 'For Christ's sake. You went to Ruth's house a couple of times and hung about throwing sheep's eyes at her. Then the third time you went you were sitting having a cup of tea in front of the fire together when you had the good luck to utter some damn fool pomposity that made her laugh. She was already quite aware of what you wanted, and she must have been turning it over in her mind. When you made her laugh, it must have just tipped the scale, and wham! you were in a clinch on the sofa.'

Keep it up, Fredric, keep it up. You're being very revealing. About yourself, not about me.'

'All right, I'll be revealing about you for a change. You're on tenterhooks at the moment. She's keeping you at arm's length and all you can think of is when you're going to get your chips. She's as good as told you that you *will* get them, but you're disappointed. Disappointed that she didn't come across with it there and then, with the kid asleep upstairs and her husband about to come home and walk in on you. So you've got one question that's eating into your mind like acid, and it's the only thing you want to talk about. *Does she sleep with her husband or doesn't she?* That's the plain question, isn't it? So isn't it time you were a bit more honest with yourself about the whole thing? You disguise it with all this stuff about how she's two-thirds wrapped up in him, and she makes an extraordinary impression, and all that. But all you care about is how soon you're going to get it, and how long it'll go on for.'

They had quickened their pace, as if to correspond with their mounting tempers. George Links, becoming aware that they were almost running, slowed down abruptly; Captax blundered on for a few steps before doing the same, and they went on in single file.

'Well, go on,' George Links snapped, glaring at the back of Captax's neck. Captax needed a haircut, and the thick, greyish-pink column of his neck was irregularly draped with shaggy tufts. As George Links noticed this, he felt his temper ebbing away. 'Go on,' he repeated in a more normal voice.

'I've finished,' said Captax gruffly, without turning round.

'That can't be all you've got to say.'

'It is all.'

'Well, then, let me go on with my story. You can't see how inadequate your summary is until you have the facts.'

Captax walked on for a dozen paces before answering. 'All right, if it pleases you. I don't care whether you tell me or not, but if it'll satisfy you, go ahead.'

As he spoke he gave a contemptuous shrug which made his head, seen from behind, settle into his shoulders amid a frill of sheepdog-like hair. The effect struck George Links as so comic that, as he struggled to contain his laughter, he felt an impulse of affection for Captax. He would have liked to pat his tousled head and call him 'good boy'.

'Don't be waxy, Fredric,' he said, overtaking Captax and patting him on the shoulder. 'I oughtn't to have taken offence when you were doing your best.'

'My best be damned. I was just saying what anybody with any common sense would have——'

'Anyway, let me tell you. She settles herself down and begins to talk in this monotone. All about Edward. And to cut it short, she gives me the key as to why he's so remote and withdrawn. You know, *inward*. It isn't just meditation. It's *conflict*.'

Captax was giving no sign of attention, but he now said, as if guardedly prepared to show some interest, 'What's he got to be in conflict about, anyway?'

'That's just it. It's his book.'

'What book? A new one he's working on?'

'Not a bit of it. *The Discovery of Faith*.'

'*The Discovery of Faith?* — But why? He's finished that — it's been out for years. All he's had to do for

59

at least a dozen years is to hold out his hand for the money.'

'That's just it. It's the money he's having the conflict about. He doesn't know what to do with it.'

'Why not, for God's sake?' asked Captax in amazement. Abandoning his pretence of not attending, he stopped dead and turned to face George Links.

'Exactly, for God's sake,' said George Links, enjoying the *dénouement* of his story. 'You hit the point there, without knowing it. He's lost his faith.'

'Lost his faith?'

'Yes, my boy. You've heard of people doing that, haven't you? Well, it's happened to the celebrated author of the *Discovery* of same. The book hadn't been out more than three years when old Cowley began to have serious doubts about the system he'd struck such a mighty blow in defence of. He wasn't the man to stifle them, so by degrees he withdrew his energies from everything else and began to devote them to wrestling with the problems involved. He didn't do any other work, but that was all right at the time because they were still living on the bounce from the book, which was considerable.'

'I'll bet it was considerable,' said Captax, his eyes lighting up with envy. 'All those cheap editions and broadcasts! Why, it's still——'

'Exactly. Well, after about twelve months in the spiritual wilderness, he suddenly came out with a bang on the other side. Informed her one morning, as soon as she opened her eyes, that he'd snapped the final link in the chain and from then on she was to consider herself married to an agnostic. He'd reached that stage at about three in the morning, apparently, and lay on his back waiting till she woke up about five hours later. That's what he's like.'

'Very nice too,' said Captax, 'except that a woman like Ruth would probably *prefer* to be woken up now and again — after all, she's——'

'I know what you're going to say. It seems he's quite satisfactory from that point of view, actually. *Or was.*'

'What do you mean, *or was*? Has he had an accident?'

The short afternoon was fading out, and their walk had brought them to the end of the Heath.

'Let's go in somewhere and get a cup of tea,' said George Links. 'I'll tell you the rest while we have it. I've got to go to my man at five, anyway.'

'Good God, you don't still go to him, do you?'

'What d'you mean, *still*? I've only been going about a month.'

'Well, are you getting anything out of it?'

They entered a tea-shop. 'Well, I never think about it much, tell you the truth,' said George Links, sitting down. 'I find my thoughts pretty much occupied with Ruth and one thing and another . . . I just accept the analysis as a necessary evil. The man says I'll benefit from it when it begins to work, and I just take his word for it. Naturally I'm——'

'Well, damn it,' said Captax impatiently, 'cut it out and have that much extra time and money to put into chasing Ruth. It's no good half-doing a thing like that.'

He broke off to order tea and toast. When the waitress had gone, George Links leaned forward and stared at him.

'Do you know, Fredric,' he said, speaking slowly and with an inflection of wonder in his voice, 'that incredible as it may seem, absolutely and utterly incredible as it is *certain* to seem——'

'You hadn't thought of that.'

'No, I hadn't,' said George Links, sitting back and gazing round him as if seeing the world for the first time.

'I'm not surprised,' said Captax briskly. 'It's always struck me how muddled people are about a situation when they're actually in the thick of it. An outside observer always has more of a grip on the thing.'

'Well, all right,' said George Links, smiling impishly. 'I'll take your advice, and in return I'm prepared to give you my hints on how to get somewhere with Barbara Bone.'

Captax sat up very straight and gave George Links a dignified stare.

'Would you mind telling me what the bloody hell you're——'

'Oh, come off it,' George Links cried, delighted at this reversal of rôles.

'No, I mean it,' said Captax, flushing dully. 'I want to know just what's given you the idea that I'm chasing the Bone woman.'

The waitress, as he spoke, was setting out the tea-things. She threw Captax a look of mingled wonder and sympathy, evidently wondering what bone woman he was chasing.

'Please remember one thing, George,' he went on, oblivious of her presence. 'I haven't consulted you about my affairs of the heart and I don't intend to.'

'It wouldn't do any harm to have an impartial comment from time to time. It would help to clarify it for you.'

'Speak for yourself. My affairs aren't in the same mess as yours.'

'Who says mine are in a mess?'

They stared at each other coldly as the tea stewed in the pot between them.

.   .   .   .   .

Dear Mr. Volumis, George Links wrote. *I am sorry to be under the necessity of breaking off my analysis before we have really got into full swing, but unfortunately . . .*

.   .   .   .   .

He posted the letter on his way home from work. That was that. All he had to do was intercept the answer, when it came. That would be easy enough; he was used to it.

Rain swirled down the High Street. The little town had settled into its hibernation. George Links sometimes wondered, fancifully, whether the hours of daylight were not even shorter in the country than in town. The trees, fields and hedges, no less than the animals, seemed to resent the intrusion of the light with its December pallor; darkness was the proper element for winter, and they gave the impression of clinging to it, trying to reduce the daylight to one irrelevant blink in the middle of the day. The paths slept dully under mud; the canal was a dark plank of liquid. Thank goodness he had some warmth, some light inside him to set against it all!

At the thought of warmth his mind, glancing off the image of Ruth, ricocheted on to Janet. He felt benevolent. Janet was a good girl. She was a good wife to him. She had been remarkably docile of late; ever since, in fact, he had fallen in with her wishes and gone to consult Volumis. Trudging along, he smiled to himself in the darkness. Well, she was quite right. The result had been a tonic; he felt it. Even if the situation had not worked out within the letter of Janet's request, he felt virtuously that it was well within the spirit. He was much more buoyant lately: he felt it in everything he did. Now that the citadel was within sight — and by God, it *was* in sight; Ruth could hardly hold out much longer in view of everything she'd conceded last time . . .

He walked up his garden path with a springy step, gaily turned the key in the door, and, entering, intercepted Janet as she was crossing the tiny entrance hall. With the unseasonable elation still on him, he did not resist the impulse to grab her round the waist and bestow, simultaneously, a kiss on the cheek and a smack on the rump.

'You're not usually so skittish of an evening,' she said, backing away wide-eyed.

'*Used* not to be,' he corrected her gaily. 'But these are new times. I really feel as if a load had been lifted from me.' He spoke in all sincerity. Ruth! he was singing inwardly. Ruth! Ruth!

'George darling, I'm so glad.'

'I bet you are. I must be miles better to live with.'

Her smile died away. 'Not *all* the time, of course.'

'No?'

'No. I don't know whether you're aware of it, but you go up and down a lot. Since you started your analysis, you've been through some — what shall I say? Some very strongly marked phases.'

Strongly marked phases! You're right, I have. He felt he was going to burst out laughing.

'Never mind,' he said, taking off his coat and going to hang it up. 'It'll all work out.' He put his arm around her waist and drew her with him into the sitting-room. Arriving on the hearth-rug, he turned her face towards him and kissed her again.

'George!' She was flushed with happiness, and bright-eyed. 'D'you know how long it is since you treated me like this?'

'The more fool me,' he said, setting about her more vigorously. Pulling her down on to the sofa, he took her in his arms, reflecting as he did so that, in some respects, her body was startlingly like Ruth's. In others, it was quite different; contrasting, indeed. He became aware that both the differences and the similarities gave him intense pleasure.

'My Janet,' he said softly. With gentle fingers he disengaged her glasses from behind her ears and took them off. Immediately the good bone structure of her face became more apparent; for the first time for years, he looked at her attentively.

'You're wonderfully good-looking.'

'You're certainly acting as if you thought so, kind sir.'

'Not as convincingly as I intend to.'

The evening passed pleasantly for both of them. Eleven o'clock found George Links comfortably in bed, glad to be there, glad to have Janet beside him, pleased

with his life and the direction it was taking, and altogether comfortable in mind and body.

'It's too early to go to sleep. Let's talk a bit,' he said
lazily.

'What shall we talk about?'

'Anything you want to.'

She stirred, a little uneasy.

'Don't move, darling, just when we've achieved the
most comfortable position.'

'Well, can we talk about something serious?'

'How serious?'

'Oh, nothing *horrible*.'

'Nothing about money, or your relatives, or repairs
to the house?'

'No. At least only very slightly about money.'

'How can it be *slightly* about money?'

She stirred again. It struck him that she seemed to
have become tense, compared with the easy, natural
way she had moulded her shape to his even five
minutes before.

'Janet, what's the matter?'

'I want you to let me have a talk with Volumis.'

'A talk with Volumis?' Careful now. No panic.
Relax those muscles, or she'll feel it.

'Yes, darling. I've been rather hesitating to mention
it, because I thought you'd think I was interfering, but
I've been thinking about it all so much, and I do so
want to know how he's getting on.'

'You mean how *I'm* getting on, don't you?'

'No I don't, I mean how *he's* getting on. After all,
he's trying to explore your mind and understand you,
and you're such a complicated person, darling —
don't misunderstand me, *please*, I love you for being

66

complicated, but well . . . I suppose I'm the person who knows you best, after all, and——'

'You want to see if his casebook contains the same kind of comment on me as yours does.'

'Oh, George darling, how *hard* you are . . . you know I'm not trying to analyse you or treat you like a patient, not in *any* way, sweetie, but it all *matters* so much to me, and I'm sure if I had just one talk with the man I could see whether he's on the right lines with you.'

'How could you possibly tell that?' he asked, trying to keep the note of angry contempt out of his voice.

'Oh, but of course I could, sweetheart. It's been worrying me so much — bad psychologists can ruin people, you know. They can absolutely *smash* them.'

'Yes, but surely'—he fought to keep the stiffness from his voice, but it would intrude — 'if I were being smashed you'd be able to tell soon enough.'

'I don't think so, darling, that's just it . . . look, do try to understand . . . he might be lulling you into a false calm and underneath it you might be sinking into a worse mess than ever.'

'Thank you for the word *mess*.' George Links hated his own voice as he heard it come out; it was the voice of a spoilt, sternly self-pitying child. 'All right, then, I shan't play and I shall tell Miss Harrison you're not playing fair.' Watch it, he told himself, for God's sake *watch it*.

'You're so hard,' her voice came faintly; she had taken her head away from his shoulder and pushed her face deep into the pillow, as if in despair. 'What does it matter about this word and that word? You know I love you and I only want . . .'

That's true, George Links thought. *She does love me.*

And suddenly he found himself acting out of character. What was more, he saw himself doing it; he had the distinct sensation of standing outside himself and watching his strange behaviour. Watching it with approval, to cap everything. *That's right, go on*, his watching self murmured.

'Come here, my sweetheart . . . no, here . . . there . . . let me tell you something . . . I don't care if you do think I'm a mess. I don't care what you think as long as you love me. You want to go and see Volumis, well, go. See him as often as you like. I'll make an appointment when I'm there next. Go and see who you like, and do whatever you like, only don't stop being my little sweetheart and loving me. Here . . . come here . . . like this . . .'

'Oh, George, you are sweet to me, you are sweet to me. Darling, you make me happy, darling, you do . . .'

What the hell am I doing this for? I ought to be saving all this for Ruth. And what shall I do when the time really comes for her to go and see Volumis?

The questions buzzed in his head, but they buzzed faintly, and presently died away altogether, leaving behind them nothing, not even the slightest residue, to tarnish the splendid bright fact that Ruth was somewhere else and Janet was here.

★ VI ★

THE saloon bar was very full, and George Links did not at first see Captax, who was standing in a corner with his back to the door. He was talking, as George Links saw with a sinking heart, to Barbara Bone and her husband, Evan.

'Hello,' he said, going up to them.

'Hello,' they raggedly chorused.

'Anybody ready for another drink while I'm getting myself one?'

'Yes, I am,' said Evan Bone promptly.

'You, Barbara?' he asked, pointedly.

'No, thanks, I still haven't anything like finished this,' she said, casting down her eyes demurely. He could not tell whether this was with a touch of womanly shyness at his use of her christian name, or whether she was glancing down at her feet to make sure they were protected by stout shoes.

'You, Fredric?'

'Thanks.' He handed over his glass. 'I'll have the usual.' They knew each other's habits.

'So will I,' said Evan Bone.

'Got a glass?'

'It's not empty yet.'

'Oh? Are you sure you want another drink, then?'

'Yes, please,' said Bone with quiet offensiveness. 'I'll have finished this by the time you get back.'

George Links shot him a glance before turning away to the bar. He was holding his long body tensely upright, head thrown back in a challenging way. A sneer gripped his thin face.

Good Lord! George Links thought. *If ever I saw a man who hated me, he does!*

He ordered the drinks, and watched while they were poured out.

But why on earth should he?

'Five shillings, please.'

'Thank you. No, I can manage, thanks. Here you are, men.'

Captax thanked him; Evan Bone accepted his in silence.

They settled into their places. If there had been a conversation in progress when he arrived, his presence seemed to have wilted it pretty effectively. Captax seemed to have withered inwards, leaving a mere exterior shell to face the world; the male Bone stared straight ahead of him, the female seemed overcome with shyness.

George Links bore it as long as he could, and finally turned to Barbara Bone.

'You're very silent this evening.'

'I think we all are,' she said, her voice scarcely audible.

'She's afraid you'll pull her shoes off if she speaks to you,' said her husband, truculently, leaning forward.

George Links put his glass down and stared at all three of them in turn. 'For God's sake,' he said. 'What's the matter with all of you? What d'you mean, she's afraid I'll pull her shoes off? You can't have taken seriously all that . . .'

'When a joke's in *that* sort of taste,' said the male Bone, 'it deserves to be taken seriously.'

'What d'you mean by that?' put in Captax, unexpectedly.

'I mean that if a man's idea of a joke is to pull women's shoes off, and tell them he's a perverted sex maniac, the chances are he's unconsciously speaking the truth.'

'Why unconsciously?' said Captax stubbornly.

'Now, listen to me,' George Links began, half rising from his seat; but he stopped in amazement. Someone was kicking him, gently but persistently, under the table. Someone with a light, graceful foot. He looked round swiftly, but even so he was only just in time to catch the appealing glance thrown him by Mrs. Bone in the instant that she lowered her eyes once more.

'Don't start a quarrel, *please*,' said the glance. 'You and I understand each other — why should we care about the others?'

He lowered himself on to the bench again, waving his hand feebly to damp the situation down. 'Oh, let it go, let it go,' he said.

'Aren't you annoyed with me for saying you must be a sex maniac?' demanded the male Bone.

'Not particularly.'

'It must take a lot to annoy you.'

'It doesn't take much from some people.'

Evan Bone turned pale with rage. 'Meaning that I'm not important enough to annoy you?'

Captax got up and began to put his coat on. 'I must go, sorry,' he muttered and immediately started for the door. George Links, without waiting to say anything to either Bone, hastily followed him.

'What the hell's going on?' he demanded, falling into step with Captax as they marched down the wet lamplit street.

'Going on where?'

'With those two, of course. Why is that Bone man so enraged with me?'

Captax walked on without saying anything. George Links began to wish it were not too dark to see his face.

'Fredric, you're acting as if you had something to hide.'

'Am I?'

They had reached another pub. George Links pushed open the door. 'Look, come in here. We can't walk about the streets.'

'I must get along. I'm busy.'

Fear clutched at George Links's heart at the thought that he might be robbed of his one possible confidant. He held the door open doggedly.

'No, look, Fredric, for God's sake don't go. Just come in here for a bit. I must talk to you.'

Captax hesitated. 'You only want to grill me about the behaviour of the Bone couple.'

'Come in if you're coming in, flippin' well,' said a peevish-looking man sitting just inside the door. 'If you're not, let go of the flippin' door.' There was a murmur of agreement throughout the bar.

George Links let the door swing to, and they walked round the corner of the building to the saloon bar. This time he bundled Captax unceremoniously over the threshold.

'Now listen, Fredric. Sit down. Wait here till I get you a drink. I must talk to you. Not about these paltry Bones — about something important.'

'Important to you, I suppose you mean.'

'Yes, damn it, important to me. Now you sit here a moment and don't move.'

The drinks were bought and carried over. Before the glasses were half empty, George Links had explained his problem.

'If she gets anywhere near Volumis, if she even rings him up or writes to him, nothing'll stop her from getting to know the truth — that I chucked going to him weeks ago.'

'H'm. That's right, isn't it?'

'Then she'll want to know what I'm up to.'

'She will,' said Captax slowly, 'won't she?'

'So I've got to keep her away from him. Now — how?'

'Give me time,' said Captax, passing his hand over his rather bulging forehead. His eyes had receded into their caves, whence they peeped out craftily. 'Give me time.'

'Well, for God's sake think of something,' George Links moaned. 'I told her I'd fix an appointment for her to see him, and I can't go back tomorrow without——'

'Got it!' said Captax sharply, banging his fist on the table.

'You mean you've thought of something? Fredric, you're a——'

'Pray silence. Pin your ears back and listen.'

·   ·   ·   ·   ·

'All alone, Ruth?'

'For the moment, yes.'

He put down his bag and tried to kiss her. She pushed him away, firmly.

'Oh, God, you're still being awkward,' he said.

'I might say the same of you.'

Sulkily, he went into the living-room and sat down. Before following, she attended to something in the kitchen.

'Ruth, darling,' he said, taking her hands in his.

'Here it comes,' she said. 'Another attack.' There was an edge of bitterness in her voice.

'Yes, here it comes. You can't expect to avoid these attacks, Ruth. Damn it, you haven't exactly behaved like a woman who really wants to avoid any complications.'

'No, I haven't, have I?' she said dully. 'I went and put a foot over the line and you'll never let me forget it.'

'Oh, darling, do come off it,' he said, pulling her towards him. She moved lifelessly, neither resisting nor co-operating. 'Here, in this very room you told me——'

'I told you I might have my own motives for letting you make love to me. And that was all the encouragement you needed.'

'How much encouragement is a man supposed to need, with a woman as beautiful as you?'

'Dear, dear,' she said with a disillusioned little smile, 'compliments now. We're well away, aren't we?'

The wave of anger which swept through his body gave George Links the courage to reach for her waist, to claw her down towards him, to press his mouth aggressively on hers. At first her body lay stiffly against

74

his; then it slackened into acquiescence. He waited, but nothing further developed. Acquiescence showed no sign of giving place to eagerness.

He wished he could reach across the room to the light switch; as things stood now, a little softly flickering firelight would do wonders. But if he moved, the ground lost might prove irretrievable. Besides, what was the good of putting the light out when her husband might walk in at any moment?

Damn and damn and damn all these complications and difficulties. He was like a hungry man sitting at the table with a meal laid before him; all that was missing was permission to eat. Anger impelled him freshly to roughness; he crushed Ruth's uncomplaining body to his own as if trying to merge her being in his by sheer force, at the same time kissing her wildly, not caring where his kisses landed.

'Ruth, Ruth, how much longer is this going on?' he moaned, rocking her in his arms.

'Till you decide to stop it, I suppose,' she murmured.

'Oh, God . . . why do you wilfully misunderstand me always? You know I don't just mean *this* — our lying here on the sofa.'

'And what makes you think *I* do?'

He held her still, anxious not to miss any syllable she might utter. 'But Ruth — if you mean, when you say *this*, our whole situation — how can I stop it?'

'How does one generally stop things?'

He felt utterly hopeless. It was all lost, all spoilt. She was simply going to quibble and split words, on and on until all the pressure subsided again. She was never going to let him get any further. His hands fell limply to his sides.

'Oh, well . . . if you're simply not interested.'

'But I asked you a question. How does one usually bring a situation to an end?'

'By making a move, I suppose,' he said without interest. 'By moving either forwards or backwards.'

She sat up straight and looked at him. 'Very well, then.'

'Very well what?'

'Move.'

George Links lay back quietly, almost inertly. His blood seemed to have been turned into some thick, bland liquid like milk; it flowed heavily in his veins.

'How can I move? I can't go back, and——'

'Then go forward.'

He kept very still, afraid to touch her, afraid even to move his eyes. At last he whispered, 'What did you say then?'

She got up from the sofa and crossed the room. The light was out and it was she who had turned it out. The firelight was flickering as prescribed. She was back with him.

'I forgot to tell you: Edward's away to-night and Teddy's staying with his Eastern Region aunt.'

'What did you say?' he repeated. 'I mean before that about Edward.'

She bent towards him. 'You know what I said. Go forward.'

He went forward.

.   .   .   .   .

Five hours later, George Links lay awake in the darkness. The night seemed to have reached its deepest point; he found it impossible to imagine anything stirring, anywhere on the moonward side of the world. He himself was intensely conscious, his thoughts forming themselves clearly and sharply in the clean-swept centre of his mind, but even he did not feel alive. He felt more like a ghost, or more properly speaking a conscious corpse. He was conscious of a physical identity, as presumably a ghost would not be; but not of *life*, only of a dead, sharp consciousness.

Why was this? Why did not the presence of Ruth, sleeping on her side with her face turned towards him, bring him to a living man's sense of his own bodily life? She was close enough to him — jammed up against him, even, since the bed in the attic was small even for one person. He could not see her face, but he pictured it. There she lay, so near that at each respiration her breath touched his neck; her head was on the same pillow as his; but she was away in another world, the world of sleep. Within her skull was a world of unconsciousness, shot through and illuminated with unknowable dreams; within his, only that sharp, fragmented consciousness. Two skulls, the administrative centres of bodies that had, in the last few hours, plunged again and again into the deepest burning centre of mutuality . . . and now it might have been continents, rather than inches, which separated them.

All at once George Links knew what it was, the feeling that possessed him. It was loneliness.

He had never known loneliness before; he saw that now. He had known what it was to want company and not to find it, and he had applied the term 'loneliness' to this situation. But now he knew loneliness as it really exists. Ruth sleeping beside him in the warm, cramped bed, her breath trailing along his neck, and in their skulls two separate worlds that could not communicate.

Staring into the darkness, he tried to comfort himself, to reject the loneliness as an illusion produced by wakefulness and fatigue. They might not be communicating *now*, but surely . . . he ran his mind over everything that had happened since she first came to his arms at the fireside. If *that* wasn't communicating . . . !

It was useless. Honesty, the uncheatable honesty of the small hours, knocked aside the feeble defence. What she had given him, what he had given her, had been wonderful, unforgettable, supremely meaningful within its own terms. But communication it had not been. Nothing had remained. They had come together, and it was over, and he found nothing of her remaining with him. The passion she had given was as evanescent as her breath on his neck, as mindless as the warmth of the bed, as empty of meaning as the darkness in which they lay.

And fifty miles to the north-west of them, away over the huddled roofs, the lamp standards, the railway yards, beyond the dark fields and the motionless villages, Janet, too, lay awake in the empty darkness.

★ VII ★

'M R. VOLUMIS?'
'Yes,' said Captax with a polite half-bow.
'I'm Janet Links.'

'Of course, of course,' said Captax, appearing to recollect himself. 'Your husband made an appointment for you to see me . . . do come in. I'm all ready for you.'

All ready? Janet Links thought. It sounded ominous, like a dentist or chiropodist or something.

'I gather you haven't been at this address long,' she said, to make conversation, as they entered the consulting-room.

'Oh yes, I have,' said Captax. 'Lived here for years.'

'Oh? Perhaps I got it wrong. But I could have sworn George told me — surely it was always Swiss Cottage he used to go to for his appointments.'

'Swiss — oh yes!' Captax cried out eagerly. 'Oh yes, of course, I used to see George at Swiss Cottage — I used to have my consulting-rooms there — all my patients used to come to me there. Only I — when I say I've lived here for years, this is actually where I live, in this flat. And as a matter of fact' — his fluency increased rapidly after the momentary stagger — 'it was the result of a deliberate policy when I let the other place go and

79

took this on. I felt that the other arrangement, of seeing people in one place and living in the other, wasn't working properly.'

He paused and looked at her keenly. She wondered why he was not offering her a chair, but murmured only, 'No?'

'No,' said Captax decidedly. 'Of course I know a lot of analysts do it. But I felt it made too much of a divorce between my everyday thinking, my day-to-day existence as it were, and my professional work — and that's just what we're always trying to avoid.'

'Divorce?'

'No, no — that kind of split between normal activity and — well, of course, you *could* say divorce was what we were trying to avoid, too, in another sense of course ... won't you sit down?' Captax added suddenly, giving Mrs. Links another attentive look. His manner became all at once very solicitous, as if he had suddenly noticed that she was pregnant.

He considered her very attractive.

She sat down, but — he noticed with distress — kept on her hat and gloves.

'Well,' she began, 'it isn't anything very special I wanted to ask you, Mr. Volumis, only I just thought I'd feel better if I met you . . .'

'And do you feel better?' asked Captax, leaning forward keenly.

'. . . and had a word with you about George,' she finished wonderingly.

'George,' said Captax thoughtfully. 'Yes. George. You know I'm really very fond of George.'

'Yes?' she said faintly.

'I like George,' said Captax sturdily. 'In fact I quite

look forward to his visits here. He has his faults, like all of us, but . . . one of the most interesting of my patients.'

'Interesting in what way?'

'In every way,' said Captax, grandly waving a hand. 'A man very well worth any psychologist's attention.'

'I don't think I quite know what to make of that,' Mrs. Links said slowly. 'I mean, it might mean that he's just terribly neurotic, or——'

'Neurotic!' said Captax loudly, making her jump. 'He's neurotic all right. I remember when he first walked in here. I mean, when he first walked in at Swiss Cottage. *Well, old chap,* I thought, *you look pretty collected on the surface, but I can see you're as neurotic as they come.*'

He paused, and Janet Links looked at him coldly. 'Is that all you've got to say?' she asked.

Captax laughed brassily. 'Good heavens, no. I'm only just beginning.' She waited, but he said nothing more.

'Well?'

'Well . . . listen, would you mind lying down on the couch?'

'Lying down on the . . .'

'Yes. You see, I rather wanted to test your . . . it's important to me to have some idea of your psychotic difficulties too. You see, George has told me——'

'What has George told you? Has he been making out that everything's my fault?'

'Oh no, nothing like that,' said Captax, smiling benignly. 'In fact, from George's account of his relations with you, the thing that emerged most strongly was that you must be exceptionally well adjusted.'

He stopped, annoyed with himself. It was no use getting the girl too complacent about her marriage. In fact, it would probably do her all the good in the world if she . . .

'That is,' he went on, 'the trouble strikes me as being mainly on George's side. In other words, you see . . . well . . . let's say you're very well adjusted to him, but he's not at the moment very well adjusted to you. Or you can put it the other way round, if you find it easier to grasp like that.'

'I don't think I quite . . .'

'Well, look. Here's this man George Links, married to a very attractive wife. In fact, I'd go so far as to say that a man like him doesn't deserve such an attrac- tive——'

'What do you mean, a man like him?'

'A man as neurotic as he is,' said Captax. 'If you ask me, he's not really capable of appreciating you. That's the basic trouble, as I see it. In a word, it's not his problem, it's yours.'

'Mine?'

'The problem of being fully appreciated,' said Captax. 'You see, George is engaged in pursuing a withdrawal-spiral.'

'A what?'

'A withdrawal-spiral. The subject gets emotionally deflected by some imperfectly-realized infantile regres- sions, and the next thing he's pursuing one mirage of withdrawal after another. He wants to spiral down- wards, only he thinks of it as *upwards* of course, into a state of complete withdrawal from ordinary human contacts.'

'But if you can see that in him, surely you can do something to stop it.'

Captax got up from his chair and began to walk gravely up and down the hearthrug.

'To stop it. To decelerate and finally to arrest it. Well, yes. But this is where I have what I'm afraid, Mrs. Links, will be a disappointment for you.'

She waited.

'A disappointment,' said Captax again. 'You see, it's a long process. Breaking into a withdrawal-spiral is one of the longest processes known to psycho-analysis. It's a question, to start with, of finding a point at which it's feasible to break in.'

'Yes?'

'Yes. And it's not always easy. When, after a fairly thorough study of the subject's temperament and background, we find ourselves still lacking a clue to this feasible intervention-point — well, then the only thing to do is to make one. We have, in other words, to make some kind of breach in the disassociated wall of consciousness.'

'A breach?' Janet Links faltered.

'By a violent emotional shock,' said Captax. He stopped pacing and stared at her grimly.

Janet Links looked round helplessly. It was all so different from anything she had imagined. Her idea of a psycho-analyst's consulting-room was derived from cartoons in the comic papers, which always showed a bare, rather clinical room with a framed certificate on the wall. Now, in her uncertainty, she found herself glancing about for the certificate. There did not seem to be one; and, though she realised that the cartoons only showed the certificate to make it clear that this *was* a consulting-room, she was conscious, faintly, of disappointment. The whole impression of the room was so — so lived-in, somehow. Captax was short of ward-robe-space, and a dark brown suit of his was hanging up on the wall; his overcoat and dressing-gown hung from pegs on the door. The kitchen door was shut, but Janet Links had the distinct impression that if she pushed it open she would see the sink full of dirty crockery. (In this she misjudged Captax, who was too lazy to cook for himself and consequently never used any crockery except a cup and saucer.)

It wasn't that the room was untidy . . . it was just that it was so *unclinical*. But he had explained about that. She felt impelled to ask him to explain again.

'You say you moved from another address to here?'

'Eh? No, no,' said Captax, a wary look coming into his eyes. 'I used to have my consulting-room at a separate address, only, as I was telling you, I wanted to bring it into line . . . listen, are you sure you wouldn't like to lie down on the couch?'

'But what would be the point?'

'Relaxation. Your responses would flow more freely.'

'But what do you want my responses to flow freely for?'

'What do you think?' Captax asked abruptly.

There was a pause. The conversation seemed to have been axed. Fuming with himself for having said anything so unfitted to his assumed character, Captax nevertheless hoped she would accept it as a piece of harmless eccentricity. His best hope, since he could not guarantee to make similar slips now and again, was to get her to see him as a psychologist of great brilliance who had an excusably non-professional manner. He began barking at her with what he hoped was amiable abruptness, cutting his sentences very short.

'Look at it this way,' he rapped out. 'You come in here. Husband a patient of mine. Severe withdrawal-spiral case. Now. Expect me to do something about it — I can only do it if I have co-operation.'

She stared at him numbly. Why had he suddenly become so different?

'Difficult type, George,' said Captax, nodding his head jerkily. 'Worth taking trouble over. But I'll tell you something, Mrs. Links.' He jabbed his finger towards her. 'We've got to work together. Essential co-operation. And another thing. I shall need to see you again.'

'Oh?'

'Yes, I shall need to see you fairly frequently,' said Captax, briskly sitting down at his desk and opening a large diary. 'Because' — and he raised his eyes to hers with a winning smile that belied the gruffness of his tone —'you know what? *You're* his best doctor. Not me — you.'

This was the way, he thought. Get her coming in regularly, and who knows? Pleased with his new rôle, he determined to keep it up; his voice became gruffer and more staccato than ever.

'Now, put it this way. Here's this man in the grip of a withdrawal — excuse me.'

The telephone was ringing. Impressively, he whipped it up to his mouth and barked, 'Captax here.'

Christ!

The telephonic voice was quacking away, but he missed several sentences in his agitation.

Had she noticed? He glanced at her, but there was no sign of suspicion on that face. It was quite possible that she had simply not registered the name. She would take it for granted that on lifting the receiver he would say 'Volumis', and, with her thoughts busy with other things, it was *possible* . . .

But *Christ*! He would have to be careful. He found himself sweating and trembling.

'Hullo, are you there, Fredric?' It was Barbara Bone speaking. 'Have you fainted or something?'

'Yes, yes, I see,' he said coolly, as if taking charge of some emergency. He was too flustered to make the additional effort of relating his answers to her questions.

'See? What d'you see? What on earth's the matter?'

'Don't shout,' he said irritably. It was the wrong thing to say, but he was afraid Janet Links would hear; Mrs. Bone's voice was terribly penetrating, even on the telephone.

'I'm not shouting. What's the matter? Are you drunk or something?'

Janet Links stirred in her seat; damn it, she *must* have heard that.

'A fractious patient,' he said, glancing up at her with a forbearing smile, and taking care to cover the mouth-piece as he spoke. 'Sometimes when they get to this stage they do—— Hello! Are you there?'

'Yes, of course I'm here. Are you ready to start attending to what I'm saying? Were you asleep?'

'Listen.' Captax switched to a sweetly-reasonable voice. 'Why don't you just ring off now and leave it all till you come for your next session? I mean, I can see you're very excited and distressed, but believe me, it'll sort itself out. Leave it till you come — I assure you the situation won't develop before then.' He heard her voice quacking madly, but talked on blandly, drowning protests, demands for an explanation, and finally sheer yelps of anger, in the steadily running eagre of his speech. 'Just ring off now, and go and take your tablets and lie down. In the morning you'll find yourself much calmer, and if you aren't, well, you can always ring me again, can't you?' He smiled patiently into the receiver. 'Good-bye, then.' Hanging up in the middle of a demented squawk, he turned to face Mrs. Links.

She was sitting composedly, with eyes downcast, as if merely thinking her own thoughts while waiting for him to deal with the interruption. But what were her thoughts? The question was, had she heard him say 'Captax' or had she not?

'Now, Mrs. Links——' he began, with a weary effort to get back into the bark-and-bluster manner. Then the telephone began shrilling again.

'Oh, God,' he moaned, sinking back in his chair. It was hopeless. How was he to keep up even the thinnest pretence of being an efficient professional psycho-analyst, when this sort of thing kept happening?

'Aren't you going to answer it?' said Janet Links; rather archly, he thought — or was that just his imagination?

'No, let it ring,' he said. But ought a genuine mental healer to be so heartless? 'At any rate — that is — look, Mrs. Links, I feel it wouldn't be worth prolonging this particular interview. The time doesn't seem very auspicious, somehow.' He raised his voice over the insistent ringing. 'I mean there are a number of things we shall have to go into. I need a lot of co-operation from you. So what d'you say to fixing another time now, and just . . .'

'But,' she objected, 'I haven't asked you *anything* yet
— surely we could get *something* settled after all the
long journey I've had to make. I mean——'

'Oh, but we have got something settled,' he shouted,
feeling that his head would explode with the monoto-
nous shrilling. He rose and opened the door for her.
'I don't suppose you realise how valuable even this
short interview has been to me. It's helped me a lot
in sizing up the situation.' Would the person never
ring off? It must be blasted Mrs. Bone, blast her. 'And
as a matter of fact, I've got as far as I feel I *can* get, on
this first meeting.'

'But how many meetings do you think——'

'Oh, lots.' He was still holding the door open. 'We
shall need to meet fairly regularly, as long as George is
in the acute stage.' (*Dring, dring; dring, dring; dring,
dring.*) 'Shall we say a week to-day at the same time?'

She was on her feet, looking at him uncertainly. 'Oh,
but I couldn't afford——'

'Free of charge,' he shouted. 'It's all part of what
I do for George, and he pays me, after all——' *That's
a good one*, he thought. 'This day week?' *Dring, dring.*

'Well,' she said, still uncertainly, 'if you're quite
sure it's necessary . . .'

'My dear Mrs. Links,' he said crisply, with a return
of confidence now that she was really going, and he
would be alone to collect his wits, 'if I didn't think it
was necessary I wouldn't——'

He stopped. The telephone was no longer ringing.

Janet Links paused in the doorway. 'That person,
whoever it was, seems to have decided to leave you in
peace. Shall I stay just a little longer? I wanted to
ask you——'

'No, really,' said Captax desperately. He was too rattled; it was essential to get her out before he made some fresh terrible blunder. 'It's better as it is. I mean, we'd hardly have got started when that cow'd be ringing again. I mean, my patient would be ringing again. Sometimes they get very troublesome.' He felt the sweat starting out on his face. 'So good-bye for now, Mrs. Links, and very nice to — I look forward to——' The telephone started again. He gestured helplessly. 'You see what I——?' She nodded and went out. He stood for a moment watching her go, then, with a surge of relief, called 'Next week!' down the stairs, hurried back into the flat and slammed the door behind him.

The telephone had barely rung six times before he had it in a murderous grip and was bawling, 'Yes? What the bloody hell is it now?'

'Thompson's garage,' said a voice. 'Your car's ready.'

'Thanks,' said Captax. 'Thank you very much indeed.'

'Don't bloody well mention it,' said the voice.

.   .   .   .   .

The saloon bar was very full, and George Links did not see Captax. But as he stood uncertainly looking about him an arm was slipped through his.

'Escort me,' said Mrs. Bone coquettishly. 'Over to the corner.'

Precise as ever, George Links speculated analytically on the nature of his feelings as they walked across the room. They were pyramidal, he decided. The basic layer was irritation; he wanted urgently to consult Captax, to get his version of the interview with Janet, and here was this tiresomely insistent little baggage, who would claim his attention and create all kinds of complications. These complications formed the theme of the second layer of his feelings. Where she was, her husband was, and if she persisted in her flirtatious behaviour the fellow's crazy jealousy would soon smoulder into flame. George Links sighed; but even as he did so, the light firm pressure of her arm through his reminded him that at the apex of his pyramid there was a small, half-formed nugget of sexual attraction and gratified vanity.

They sat down. Barbara Bone was pretty; he had to grant that, in the silent debate that went on inside his head. What was more, she was looking at him in a way that offered every encouragement. If he had been interested in her, what a triumph this would represent! What a stupefyingly rich reward, for almost no effort!

She said nothing; asked for no drink, broached no topic, simply looked at him steadily and with a faint, half-menacing smile.

Well, why wasn't he interested? *What was he waiting for?*

Forgetting everything else, George Links leaned forward with his elbows on the table and applied his entire concentration to this problem. He stared at Mrs. Bone. Here she was, undeniably very decorative, equally undeniably giving him the signal to proceed. *Why was it so meaningless?*

'Why don't you say something?' she asked, suddenly.

'I don't know what to say.'

She pondered a moment, then: 'Is that because you can't decide what you'd *like* to say? Or do you know what you'd like to say and don't know whether to say it because of what I might think?'

How easy she was making it! She seemed determined to spare him any kind of donkey-work; even the minor embarrassments and uncertainties, incidental to this kind of situation, were brushed aside by her blunt questioning.

Well, why not be a clever opportunist — a cad, in short? Why not take what was going, even when it came thick and fast? Goodness knows, it all helped to counterbalance the thin times — and there had been, and doubtless would be in future, plenty of *them*.

He opened his mouth to make some suitable answer to her archly provocative questioning; something on the lines of, 'I certainly know what I'd *like* to say, and when you look at me so sweetly I feel inclined to risk it.' That formula would be good enough to pave the way for the next step.

'I certainly——' he began.

She waited, but it was all.

'You certainly . . . ?' she prompted.

He lowered his eyes, stared at the table, shook his head morosely. It was no use.

Ruth! You've got me . . . damn you!

With a kind of stubborn idiocy he continued to shake his head, as if not merely the power but the will to speak had left him.

He felt her hand on his. 'George, what's the matter?'

How *tender* her voice was! All the raillery, all the challenge, had gone out of it. In an instant she had become all gentleness, all concern. Probably she was blaming herself for not assessing the situation more accurately, not seeing that he was genuinely in love with her, genuinely suffering the stress and sway of profound emotion.

He wanted to laugh, to be sick, to hide himself, to slap her, to kiss her, all at the same moment.

His one chance . . . his one chance to play the rôle of successful cad, buoyant heartless amorist, spry collector of trophies. It was a part he had often understudied in his dreams, hoping that one day by some twist of circumstance he would be called on to play it — and here it was, tossed into his lap. And useless to him, useless. An emotion he had always sought to deny — the obsessive wish to possess one woman, making any other adventure seem impossibly drained of meaning — had caught and was holding him.

Her hand slipped away from his. 'Be careful,' she said in a low voice.

Careful? Why?

'Here you are, then,' said Evan Bone's voice. It had a bright, hard edge to it, George Links thought. But no; accuracy in all things; it was not so much an *edge* as a *surface*. A bright hard surface, like a knuckle-duster.

'Yes, here we are,' said George Links, trying to keep perfectly still in his seat, but aware of an almost uncontrollable impulse to jump up and fall into a defensive position. Evan Bone, standing tensely over him, had exactly the air of a man about to lash out first and ask questions afterwards.

Evan Bone, without moving his face, allowed his eyes to wander to the bare expanse of table between his wife and George Links; bare except for an ash-tray and an empty sherry-glass left by some previous customer.

'Been here long?' he asked coolly.

'About five minutes.'

'Five minutes, eh?' Bone raised his eyebrows and nodded his head at the same time, conveying that he registered this extraordinary and significant fact. 'Five whole minutes and you haven't got round to getting a drink yet. Looks as if you had plenty to talk about.'

'How d'you know we weren't simply waiting for you and Captax to turn up?'

As soon as the words were out, George Links knew that he had made a bad move. Evasiveness of that kind could do nothing except put him in a false position.

The Bone man was staring at him even more grimly, ostentatiously not troubling to answer his question.

It was all too absurd. The consciousness of virtue — a virtue obliquely arrived at, but still genuine — flooded George Links's veins. Abruptly, he stood up.

'Look here, I can see perfectly well what you're getting at, and I've had enough of it.'

'Oh no, you haven't,' said Bone, nastily shaking his narrow head. 'You haven't had anything like enough of it. You're just beginning.'

Barbara Bone, who had been watching the scene inertly, seemed suddenly to realize that it concerned her. She gave a loud yelp of 'Evan — *please*——'

'Be quiet,' he said to her, making the words as much as possible like a slap across the face.

'I won't be quiet. You're just making a ridiculous——'

'Barbara, go home.'

'I won't——'

'*Go home!*' he shouted. Silence fell, and every head in

93

the bar turned towards them. Only the wireless went on singing to itself gaily and insanely.

George Links felt, as in a nightmare, that the situation had leapt into a dimension where he was powerless to control it. But the sight of the tear that rolled down Barbara Bone's cheek did what her coquetry had failed to do: it brought him in uncompromisingly on her side.

'Oh, leave her alone, Bone,' he snapped. Damn the fellow's name! — it had ruined the dignity of his protest by forcing him into that absurd jingling rhyme. Still, he must go on. 'If you want to pick a quarrel with me, that's all right, but——'

'It certainly is all right,' Bone said loudly, turning on him with a fresh blaze of resentment. 'I'm going to pick one, don't worry. I just don't see why Barbara should be in on it, that's all.'

'Well, for that matter, the whole lot of us will be out in the street if you do any more of that shouting,' said George Links, still casting about for some means of getting the situation back on to a calmer level.

'And I'm not sure that isn't the best place for us. The sort of thing I feel like saying to you would be out of place in a quiet, respectable public-house.'

George Links, whose precisian's ear registered the penultimate word as 'pullic' rather than 'public', now realized that Bone had been drinking. Gaining Dutch courage for the encounter, evidently. If that was so, it was useless to try to discuss the matter calmly; if Bone was nerved for a scene, possibly culminating in a fight, there was nothing he could do about it except defend himself.

And yet it was all so damned *pointless*!

'Look here,' he was beginning, wearily, when Barbara Bone created a diversion by jumping to her feet and starting for the door in a rapid, jerky strut that expressed her anger and embarrassment. Looking straight ahead of her, and with no word of farewell or explanation, she went through the door and out.

'Good,' said Bone unconvincingly. 'Now she's gone home we can——'

'Don't be an ass,' George Links interrupted, driven by his rising irritation. 'You don't think she's gone home any more than I do. She's just gone off to find someone to pour her troubles out to. And it won't surprise me if that someone turns out to be a man. You're just going the right way to——'

'Oh, it won't surprise you, eh? You think of her as pretty generally available, I dare say. Well, that's exactly what I——'

'Oh, don't be such a fool!' George Links felt his voice rising to a yell; his irritation was unbearable. 'You come in here and make a scene, humiliating the girl and putting her in a rage, so out she walks, leaving you still barking up the wrong tree — and all the time you're sitting here, keeping up this silly farce with me, she's off on her own in exactly the mood that's going to make her do something reckless.'

Evan Bone had sat down in the seat just vacated by his wife; leaning his elbows on the table, he faced George Links just as she had done.

'Yes,' he said, wagging his long, meagre head up and down, 'I can see that's exactly the view you'd like me to take of the matter. Don't worry, Links. I'm not underestimating your cunning.'

'My *cunning*, blast you?'

'Yes, you heard. A man who goes in for your sort of sly little game has to be cunning — and I'm quite prepared to reckon with it.'

George Links sat back in his chair. All at once a feeling of great weariness possessed him, and he began to be aware that he had not yet had a drink. Why was it all so utterly, utterly wearisome? Here was this fanatical young fool, sitting opposite him and settling down to a long bout of grilling. The man couldn't, in a way, be blamed; as he, deludedly, saw it, the most important issues were at stake; normally timid and insignificant, he had keyed himself up to the ordeal of a clash, with the deadly determination to scare this interloper away from his wife. Quite possibly, insect though he was, he genuinely loved the said wife. And, convinced by some crazy process of his own logic that George Links was really giving chase to the girl, he was out to put up the best resistance in his power.

'I want a drink,' George Links said drably, getting up. He hesitated, then added, 'I'll get you one if you like.'

Evan Bone gave no sign of having heard this offer; he sat frozen, staring at the spot where George Links's face had been before he rose from his chair.

With a shrug, George Links went over to the bar, waited his turn, and bought himself a whisky, which he tossed down immediately, and a pint of beer, which he carried over to the table and set down.

'Right, now go on,' he said. 'You're here to tell me to leave your wife alone. It's useless for me to say that I'm not doing anything else, because you've got it into your head that I'm cunning and unscrupulous.'

'*Well, aren't you?*'

Bone spoke viciously, twitching his body forward

suddenly. The effect was stronger than he could have known.

George Links put out his hand to the beer-glass, then withdrew it, then put it out again. He picked up the glass and carried it half-way to his lips, then put it down again untouched.

Cunning and unscrupulous? Well, aren't you?

Evan Bone was staring at him intently. Even though he could not have understood the force of his words, he could see that they had gone home.

'Keep right away from her, d'you hear?' he said, following up his advantage. 'I blame myself that I didn't interfere right at the start — that evening when you were fooling about with her shoes.'

George Links made no reply. The situation was too richly charged, too loaded with ironies. There was nothing he could do with it.

The drink was ebbing away from Evan Bone's brain. With each heartbeat he became more gangling, more tensely ineffectual. Even in the midst of his own situation, George Links could feel the pathos of the man who had married a too pretty wife, had married her for her prettiness, and was unsure of his power to hold her.

The conversation, at one time so full of menace, was running down. Neither of them had anything to say to the other; each sat brooding on the immense load of worries he carried inside him. George Links felt that if they sat there much longer, in their present mood, some horrible kind of sympathy would come into being; they would begin by agreeing to some idiotic proposition such as that all the problems of life were caused by the flighty behaviour of women, and go on to get drunk together and share maudlin confidences.

To evade this he said, 'I'm going now. You've made your point. You think I'm the kind of man who wouldn't scruple to seduce someone else's wife. Well, you're right. As it happens, you're wrong in the particular case of your own wife. But the way I feel at the moment, I don't feel able to derive much comfort from that.'

Even Bone raised his eyes from the table to a point about mid-way up George Links's chest, and said, 'I'm not wrong. I have my evidence.'

'As you please,' said George Links. He walked over to the door and into the street.

It was dark and windy. Rain had fallen, and the pavements were shining in a bleak way that did nothing to raise his spirits. Meanwhile, his main object was still not achieved. Where the hell was Captax?

This was intolerable. It was urgent that he find Captax and consult him immediately. He must find out how the pseudo-consultation with Janet had gone off. She had been so strangely silent on the topic — hardly referred to it at all. He had puzzled continually, that week-end, over her few and short answers to his questions, over her tone of voice and expression as she spoke, and still he was no nearer any glimpse of what was going on in her mind. Captax must speak: he must, urgently.

He saw a taxi approaching, hailed it, and gave Captax's address. Captax had been going to meet him in the saloon bar, according to their usual arrangement; was he ill, or so preoccupied by some crisis that he had forgotten?

Huddled on the leather seat, watching the lights go past the window, George Links tried to assemble the

fragments of his life into some order. He thought of
Ruth, the woman he had staked so much on; Janet,
the woman he wanted chiefly to placate, to keep happy
and unconscious of what was going on; Barbara Bone,
the woman he had drawn into the net without meaning
to — whom he had attracted, indeed, mainly by not
caring whether he attracted her or not. And the difficult
or enigmatic figures of the various men involved in the
pattern — Bone, Edward Cowley, Captax. *Captax* —
yes, what was he up to? What had Bone meant by
saying 'I have my evidence'? With a mind like his,
'evidence' was more than likely to mean some more or
less fantastic story told him by a confident bamboozler,
with not a crumb of what George Links's legal mind
would consider evidence.

How could it, indeed, be anything else? For there
was, after all, no evidence; he had never, except for his
one lapse into horseplay in the pub, overstepped the
bounds of the strictest propriety with the girl . . . God,
what a blunder *that* had been, by the way! — just the
sort of thing that would be seized on by any budding
Iago who wanted something to use as a fulcrum for
the husband's suspicions.

The taxi stopped at Captax's address. George Links
paid the driver and watched him drive away. The street
was empty, and quiet except for the fitful gusts of wind.
Captax's flat was on the second floor; there were the
stone stairs up which he must carry his questions; but
what questions? And what kind of answers did he
expect to bring down with him?

Feeling suddenly chilled and despairing, he climbed
slowly up the stairs and rang Captax's bell. There was
a long silence. He rang again. Was the man out?

Quite possible; even, in view of the circumstances, probable; and yet George Links was possessed by a strong intuition that someone was there, someone whose refusal to answer the bell was a deliberate evasion. In a fury, he jabbed at the bell-push time and time again, varying it with savage outbursts of knocking.

Ha! The door was opening. And it *was* Captax, looking angry and furtive.

'Not now, George,' he said.

'What d'you mean, not now? We had an arrangement to meet.'

'Unforeseen circumstances,' said Captax, beginning to close the door. George Links took a step forward and planted his foot inside the threshold.

'Nice technique,' Captax sneered. 'Where'd you learn that? On the road with a bag of brushes?'

'Damn your evasions. I wanted to talk to you urgently.'

'And can't you accept the fact that some things take natural priority over others?'

'You're talking like a pompous fool, Fredric. If you mean you've got a woman in there, say so.'

'Take your foot out of my door,' said Captax grimly.

'Who is it — Barbara Bone?'

'Take your foot out of my door, I said.'

'All right,' said George Links. What was the use? 'Only there's just one favour I still want to ask you. When you've finished with her, tell her husband you were lying about me, will you? And that your motive was to put him on a false scent while you——'

He had taken his foot from the door while speaking; without waiting for the conclusion of the sentence, Captax closed it, unhurriedly, in his face.

★ VIII ★

CHRISTMAS was coming, and the High Street wore
a halo of mist through which the sunlight glowed
red and gold. To Janet Links, coming out of a
department store with a basket full of parcels, it seemed
that December had never been so generous, so festive,
so full of the promise of warmth and conviviality. This
would be one Christmas that she and George were
really going to *enjoy*.

She turned out of the High Street into the quieter
road that led to their cottage. Home. How much more
point there seemed to be, nowadays, in keeping the
place going. All the cleaning and cooking and buying
things and dealing with the tradesmen — it was *worth*
doing it, now that she felt George loved her. And she
did feel it. He had been so warm, so affectionate, lately;
no woman could doubt, after the sort of demonstration
he had been giving, that she was desired and cared for
and made much of as a woman.

Gaily she tripped along, swinging her basket. The
Christmas rush hadn't started yet, and already she had
most of the presents. Everything was going splendidly —
because George loved her, George loved her. Of course
there were still one or two little mysteries to be looked
into — or not looked into, as the case might be. Why
had George arranged for his friend to put on this idiotic

masquerade? She almost burst out laughing when she remembered the ludicrous failure Captax had made of it. Why, she had known there was something wrong, that this was no analyst, long before he had rapped out 'Captax' into the telephone and then given that tremendous start. At the thought of that moment she really did burst out laughing, quite loudly. Poor Captax! She had felt quite sorry for him. And he was quite sweet, really. What could they be up to? George must have got him to do it, to keep her from going to the real Volumis. However, it didn't matter. Perhaps she ought to feel worried about it, but whenever she tried to work up any anxiety, all she could feel was the pressure of George's arms round her, as she had known it lately — so beautifully, so beautifully . . .

How could she worry about his little whims, his pathetic little conspiracies with Captax, when she had *that* kind of tangible evidence that things were all right?

She began to laugh again, with the sheer joy that welled up from the centres of her body, and as she did so she had another vision of Captax's appalled face, his glazed eyes, as he stared rigidly in front of him after blurting out his name. The one laugh, so to speak, merged into the other. How absurdly funny he was! — and how absurdly happy she felt!

Dusk had not yet begun to fall, and as Janet, still chuckling, turned the corner and came in sight of the cottage, she saw at once that a man was standing at the front door, perhaps waiting for someone to answer his knock or ring. A tall, thin figure, taller and thinner even than George . . . some friend of his? Someone come to break the news that George had slipped and fallen under a train at Paddington Station?

She quickened her pace, forgetting about Captax and Christmas. Was George all right? Or had this long, thin young man (she saw, as she got nearer, that he was young) come to tell her that he had dived into the river to save someone's life and been drowned?

She clicked open the garden gate. Evan Bone, swivelling at the sound, faced her unblinking.

'Mrs. Links?'

'Yes.'

.   .   .   .   .

George Links rolled on to his back and stared moodily at the ceiling. The attic had no curtain on its small window, and the thin, sharp 7 a.m. light had woken him. Not that he had been at all deeply asleep; indeed, it seemed to him that he could remember everything that had happened during the night, a tedious chronicle of shiftings from left to right, vague noises from the street, fishings under the pillow for his handkerchief, and patches of extra loud ticking from his watch. He had slept, but the change from waking to sleeping had been nothing more than shifts from just above the level of consciousness to just below it.

Stirring irritably, he clasped his hands behind his head. Sleep! How could he sleep with this turmoil going on in his veins? Lying there, on his back, he almost felt at that moment the physical sensation of prongs being pushed up into his body from down below, somewhere under the floorboards. Damn it, that was it! Groaning, he realized that the bedroom occupied by Ruth and her husband was immediately below where he was lying. Their room was bigger than his attic, but the indisputable, horrible fact remained that right underneath him, as he lay there, the Cowleys were sleeping. Or had they woken up? Were they murmuring to each other, listening, as he was listening, to the sharp drumming of the handfuls of rain which the wind was throwing against the window? The wind was discontented; it dashed the rain against the glass as if in a petulant attempt to wake up the household. That, at least, was what it conveyed to him: but what did it convey to them? It mirrored the discontent he already had inside him; what did they have inside them? Probably the lashing of the rain only served to emphasize the warmth, the sheer delightfulness, of being in bed. That's how it would to him, anyway, if he had Ruth in bed. Ouch! George Links actually groaned with sudden pain at the full realization of what it would be like. God, what a unique kind of pain it was . . . especially now that he knew what she was like. . . .

'Ruth,' he muttered to his pillow. 'Ruth, Ruth, Ruth, you bitch, you bitch. . . .'

A wave of pleasure and drowsiness engulfed him as, for a moment, he succeeded in fooling himself and reacting as if she were really there, really present in all her velvety richness.

'You bitch,' George Links moaned again, but this time with a note of sleepy gratification in his voice. Then he noticed that the door was opening.

Who was this? Stiffly, he lay with one eye half open, alert for anything. Had Ruth stolen out of Cowley's bed and flitted upstairs to snatch a moment with him before dressing? The thought was not even fully formed before his roving mind had contemptuously deserted it and arrived at another. It was Cowley coming to have it out with him, perhaps to murder him before anyone else was up. On the pretext of getting up to light the stove and make Ruth a cup of tea, he was going to strangle George Links, dismember him and burn the pieces in the stove while he waited for the kettle to boil. Or perhaps he was going to make a longer job of it. With a sudden flash of masochistically acute vision, George Links saw himself chained up beside a bath of acid.

These thoughts and images were contained within the two or three seconds it took the door to swing open far enough to reveal, about half-way up its length, a grave face topped by a tousled poll.

'I was going to creep in,' said Teddy, 'and get my train book without disturbing you. But when I got to the door I heard you talking.'

Did you, by God!

'Talking,' said George Links feebly. 'You sure, Teddy?'

Teddy nodded. 'I heard you saying *ditch, ditch.*'

George Links relaxed. 'I must have been talking in my sleep,' he said, smiling. 'Whatever could I have been dreaming?'

Teddy, having no contribution to make to this topic of speculation, walked sedately across the room and reached up to a shelf. He was wearing blue cotton pyjamas and carpet slippers. George Links noticed that he put his hand without hesitation on one particular cloth-bound exercise book, though the shelf contained at least a dozen, all identical, and that he stowed it under his arm without even a glance to verify its identity.

'What particular train book is that?' he asked, following with his eyes as Teddy moved over to the door. How strange the child was!

'Southern Region, second volume,' said Teddy.

Were all children as strange as this? What must it be like to be the father of one?

Teddy was at the door; he was going; he must be stopped, held, made to talk.

'Teddy.'

'Yes?'

'Are you going to read your train book now, before you get up?'

'Not read it. Write something in it.'

Not wishing to get bogged down in detail, George Links avoided asking what he was going to write.

'Will you go back to bed and write in your book till it's time to get up?'

'I shall sit by the gas fire in my dressing-gown till I hear Dad get up.'

'Does Dad always get up first?'

'*Nearly* always,' said Teddy. He suddenly looked at George Links with Ruth's serious look, the one she suddenly switched to before saying something she considered important. 'Which are you friends with most, my Mum or my Dad?'

The combined effect of the question and the sudden effect of Ruth's genetic presence completely unnerved George Links. Still, he made an effort to answer the question truthfully.

'I haven't known either of them very long, but in that time I've seen more of your mother, so I feel I know her better than your Dad.'

'So you're more friends with her than you are with him?'

'Up to now, yes,' said George Links, feeling desperation welling up inside him.

'Good,' said Teddy. 'Because you'll be able to keep her company this afternoon.'

'Keep her company?'

'Dad's taking me on a Southern Region excursion. At least, it's not an excursion for him, because he has to go anyway. But he's taking me, so it's an excursion for me. We'll be on electrified line as far as Aldershot, and then——'

'Are you going to be away long?' George Links asked above the slamming of his frightened heart.

'We're going on the 2.6 from Waterloo, and I don't suppose we'll be back before 7.10, unless we come via Guildford. The winter services are different. Some of the fast freights have prierority.'

'Priority,' George Links corrected him mechanically. But his mind was already busy with its main subject. The desire to question Teddy had suddenly evaporated. He rolled on to his back again. Clutching 'Southern Region, Volume II' under his arm, Teddy noiselessly disappeared.

Groaning, George Links writhed out from under the bedclothes and straightened up with his feet on the cold floorboards. The bed had suddenly become intolerable; the conflicting emotions inside him were roused to such frenzy that he had the most concrete physical awareness of them. They were like maddened snakes thrashing in a tin box — the box being his chest.

'What did I do?' he moaned, struggling into an old mackintosh in lieu of a dressing-gown and starting out for the bathroom. 'What was it?'

He blundered down a flight of steps and along a corridor, hardly even noticing in his clotted misery that his way led past the closed bedroom door of the

Cowleys. In the bathroom, he squirted taps, dabbed at himself, fiddled with soap, made a few ineffectual gestures with a toothbrush. It was all too much for him. The snakes were thrashing about harder than ever, and there were more of them than he had ever suspected. Teddy's visit alone seemed to have bred half-a-dozen fresh ones. Why had he never noticed that the boy had his mother's eyes? What cold, repulsive inertia in him had prevented the realization that Teddy's presence in the house was a powerful emotional focus? He had always thought of the boy, though without bitterness, merely as a nuisance, to be kept out of the way; a distraction for Ruth, a possible source of trouble. Why had he not seen the enormously complicated range of emotions that were called into being merely *because Teddy existed*?

And as for Ruth. And as for Edward Cowley. And as for the whole bloody, hopeless, torturing business. He had had enough. Not that he wanted Ruth any less. Nothing had diminished; everything had grown. His physical yearning for Ruth had stayed where it had always been — at peak — but it had been strengthened and solidified by the other emotions that had packed in round it.

'What was it?' George Links asked again. He spoke in a quiet voice to avoid being overheard, but the tension within his chest was too great to admit of his merely asking himself the question inwardly. He had to speak, to utter the words so that they struck his own ear-drums, if no one else's.

He climbed up to the attic and stood for a moment, irresolute, staring through the fitfully rinsed window, his hands plunged in the pockets of his mackintosh. A gust of ticking from his watch arrested his attention, and he went over to where it lay and took it up. 7.40. The Cowleys probably weren't even awake yet. For them the day hadn't begun. It was still last night. For another few minutes at least, he was ahead of them. The thought suddenly seemed an important one. It gave him the feeling that he had, for the moment, outrun his problems. Quick! He could dress, throw his pyjamas and sponge-bag into his grip, and be out of the house before the Cowleys' calendar caught up with his — what a deliciously contrived escape! The slam of the front door, as he left the house for ever, would probably be what woke them up. ' *There!* ' it would say. ' I'm off — *slam* — and you have my permission to move into to-day.'

Muttering to himself, George Links began feverishly making his preparations, peeling off his pyjamas, stuffing them still warm into his bag, dragging on his clothes. By the time his watch read 8.46 all was over.

He looked round the attic, telling himself that he was seeing it for the last time. Not quite all of him believed it; there was a poky, unreachable corner which knew, with serene hopelessness, that as long as Ruth lived there he would be in the offing somewhere. So he reiterated it all the more fiercely inside his head.

'Good-bye,' he said quietly to the attic. But it refused to answer.

Let it! He was out on the landing, he was going down the stairs, then down another flight of stairs, he was on the ground floor, his hand was on the front door knob.

Good-bye! Good——

'That you, Ruthie?'

Edward Cowley's voice, from the kitchen.

Well, go on! Open the door and go on out! It isn't you he's calling to, is it?

'No, it's me,' he said through the open door, quickly putting his bag and mackintosh down where they would not be noticeable.

'Oh, hullo,' said the voice, then the philosopher's huge face appeared round the door. 'You're up early. I'm just making some tea. . . . Come in the kitchen, if you don't mind the squalor.'

George Links went into the kitchen and sat down on a wooden chair as unhesitatingly as if Cowley had given orders with a gun in his hand. Cowley, wearing dungarees over his pyjamas, had nearly finished raking out the stove; the kettle, on the gas stove, was beginning to fume.

Knowing that a man employed on domestic chores is always working to a semi-automatic routine, which is hard to interrupt, George Links did not embarrass Cowley with an offer of help. He simply sat and watched while the philosopher emptied one final shovelful of ashes into the bucket, carried it out to some unknown destination offstage, came back, washed his hands, tipped a calculated amount of tea into a black china pot and poured boiling water on it.

Watched impassively by George Links, Cowley allowed the tea to stand for two minutes, part of which he occupied in setting out three cups and saucers. Then he poured out one cup and, taking the kettle, replenished the teapot with an equivalent volume of hot water.

'I'll just take Ruth's up first,' he said, going to the door with the cup in his hand.

George Links did not move or speak. There seemed

to be nothing he could do, nothing he could even want
to do. It was a complete deadlock. He liked and
respected Cowley. He also wanted to make love to
Ruth. He felt glad that he had already slept with Ruth
once. Simultaneously, at a deeper level, he revered
Cowley and felt an impulse to appeal to him, to lay all
his problems before the man in the hope that his wisdom
would be able to provide a solution that would bring
some measure of peace and happiness. At this level, he
regretted having slept with Cowley's wife, and felt
ashamed of wanting to do it again. But the levels kept
merging and fading into one another; besides, there
were other unidentifiable levels, or spots, which kept
sending out signals and jamming the others. Patches
of feeling about Teddy kept crowding into his awareness. George Links felt that he liked Teddy, loved him
indeed, and wanted to make amends for having injured
him by making his mother an adultress. On the other
hand, he also felt a kind of yearning, a reaching out
towards the boy, which made him feel glad that by
physically possessing his mother he had put himself
into something like a father's position towards him.
Wasn't it the case that if you slept with a woman you
entered into *some* kind of relationship, however tenuous,
with her children? Didn't it give him a sort of share in
Teddy? But then another patch of emotion claimed
his attention, insisting that what he really felt about
Teddy was simply an amalgam of everything he felt for
either of the parents: including the wish to possess him
(because he derived from Ruth) and the impulse to
revere him as a being of a superior order (because he
derived from Edward Cowley). Ruth, Teddy, Edward:
mother, son, husband; lover, rival, legal owner; sister,

elf, mage — would the pieces never again stand still? Would no pattern ever again emerge?

Yes; one thing was clear. He wanted to get Ruth Cowley into bed again, if only just once before he died. Solemnly, sitting upright on the kitchen chair, George Links specified this ambition to himself as the chief aim of the rest of his life-span.

Edward Cowley came down again and poured out two cups of tea. Owing to his foresight in replacing the tea poured out for Ruth with an equivalent volume of water, the second and third cups were uniform in colour and density with the first.

At last there was nothing for them to do but sit opposite each other at the kitchen table, resting their elbows on the bare, scrubbed board, drinking the tea.

George Links felt drained. The violence of his recent inner turmoil had used up so much of his strength that he was barely able to lift his teacup. Like a person rescued from a collapsed building, he sat inertly, staring in front of him, feeling that it was enough that he could breathe, and sip tea, and wait for life to begin again.

His stillness contrasted oddly with Cowley's. The two of them sat equally motionless, but Cowley gave no impression of emptiness or fatigue, only his usual one of a complete physical repose bred of mental withdrawal.

The silence broke George Links's guard first, as it naturally would. Half-way through the first cup he began to fidget; as Cowley began to pour out a second, he said, keeping his voice as level as he could, 'Teddy tells me you're taking him on a jaunt this afternoon.'

Cowley, passing across the filled cup, smiled. 'Yes. I sometimes go to spend a few hours with a philosopher friend of mine. I've never taken Teddy before, but I think now he's old enough to amuse himself while we talk' — his smile reappeared, firstly as if in apology — 'about what interests us.'

George Links felt suddenly that he must question Cowley about his beliefs, get him to talk seriously. His nagging unrest was coming back after the momentary peace of exhaustion. Surely a man so full of wisdom could communicate *something* healing, even to one whose only tangible wish was to get to bed with his wife?

'What interests you,' he said slowly, 'if I might venture to guess, would be philosophy — as it was traditionally understood rather than as practised by the philosophers who occupy the limelight at the moment.'

Cowley nodded. 'As you imply,' he said, 'I haven't much sympathy with the academic philosophy of the moment. Its real weakness seems to me a human rather than a technical one; it tends to allow a certain kind of mind to assume undue prominence.'

George Links waited a moment and then prompted, 'What kind of mind?'

'A mind like a little bright, sharp penknife. Excellent for cutting apple-peel into neat shapes, but not much use for hacking out clearings in the forest.'

'And that's how you see philosophy — that it's still, after all these centuries, a matter of hacking out clearings?'

Edward Cowley waved one hand in the gesture of a man indicating a mountain range. 'Look for yourself,' he said. 'Are any of the traditional problems of philosophy any nearer to being solved by us than they were by the Greeks? Are ethics any better understood? Are metaphysics? Does one person in a hundred thousand know what he really believes or what he really ought to do?'

George Links put his cup down and raised his eyes to Cowley's. 'No. *I* don't,' he said simply.

For a moment they looked at each other quite nakedly. George Links had the feeling that Cowley understood him perfectly, *knew*, in essence, the whole range of his being. He might have this or that secret from Cowley, there might be this or that fact that Cowley was unaware of — including, please God, his whole relationship with Ruth; but facts of this kind were, for the moment, unimportant. Cowley knew *what kind of man he was*: and a sense of relief flooded through his mind at the thought that someone understood.

'You don't,' Cowley repeated. 'And yet here you are, a clever man, a lawyer, somebody who's successful in all sorts of ways. And the one really important thing, the one thing that's capable of holding the rest together, you can admit that you don't know about: you can admit it because you know that the admission only puts you in the same boat as everyone else. You don't know, nobody knows. But at least, as long as these tremendous problems exist, it's clear enough what philosophers *ought* to be doing.'

George Links thought of *The Discovery of Faith* heaped on the bookstalls. He wanted to remind Cowley of its existence, to recall him to the fact that in the eyes of the world he, Cowley, figured as a man to whom the basic ethical and metaphysical problems were *not* problems — to whom they appeared as having been solved by revelation. But he did no more than open his mouth and close it again. To bring up the question he would have had to feign ignorance, to conceal what he knew about Cowley's massive dilemma; and it was not a time for feigning.

'I appreciate the sincerity of your concern with these problems,' he said instead. 'But what I don't understand is, where do you get the stubbornness that makes you go on? If you put the discovery of truth, or the reconciliation of irreconcilables would perhaps describe it better — if you put that in the centre of your life, and make everything else contingent on it, how do you know you're not just squandering your life? — staking it, I mean, on the desperate chance that you'll succeed where all the others have failed?'

Cowley, his elbows on the table, laid one large hand on the other. He made no other movement, not even altering the angle of his head; and yet there was no suggestion of the reptilian: the power that lay behind his stillness was as palpable as ever.

'I'm not as altruistic as that would imply,' he said. 'If you think of me as giving up my life to a search for the ultimate philosophical certainties, you have altogether too saintly a picture of me. It's not a question of trying to succeed where everyone else has failed. Because in the kind of attempt I'm making, not everyone *has* failed. Men *have* succeeded in working out certainties in the intervals of doing other things. The only difference between me and most of the others who've tried it is that I can't work out my certainties in the intervals of doing other things. I can't just let life go on and take time off now and again to ponder these questions. I'm in a state of suspended animation, and shall be until these things clarify themselves in my mind. It's a limitation in me, I know.' He spoke the last

sentence as if talking to himself, but willing that George
Links should overhear him.

George Links felt the snakes beginning to thrash
about in the tin box. One of them in particular kept
thumping its scaly tail right on his heart. Cowley must
help him, he must, he *must*.

'You speak of working out certainties for oneself,'
he said, leaning forward. 'Do you mean that these
things are all subjective? Isn't there any such thing as
truth that's the same for everyone?'

Cowley sat silent for a moment, watching the steam
wreathing upwards from his cup.

'There is such a thing,' he said at last. 'But human
beings are so embedded in their own individual selves
that they view it from such different angles. The only
bit of the human mind that's more or less the same for
everybody is the reason. That's why philosophers have
always overestimated rationality, put so much faith
in it that they've made the search for truth into a
child's game with counters. A man apprehends truth
with his whole personality. So his first duty is to come
to terms with that personality — to assess what his
equipment will enable him to do. Then he can approach this objective pinnacle of truth with the aim of
mapping as much of it as he can get at. When he's
reached the limits of what he can get at — when he
can say that he's grasped everything his temperament
will permit him to grasp, and tested it all against his
total experience of life — then he can begin to talk
about what he believes.'

'You make believing sound very hard,' said George
Links.

'It is very hard. That's what Blake meant when he

said, "Many people are not capable of a firm persuasion of anything".'

'You don't think one can hold — as it were — provisional beliefs?'

'If your temperament will permit the amount of self-deception and stalling that they involve, yes.'

George Links drew in his breath sharply. The answer came to him like a bump against granite. There it was, the difference between himself and Cowley. For *his* temperament did permit self-deception and stalling, even at the cost of having snakes thumping at his heart. Cowley was an all-or-nothing man; he was a something-and-everything man.

'Do you believe,' he said slowly, 'that *everything* in a man's make-up, every element of his total personality, has its contribution to make towards his vision of truth?'

'Everything that makes for awareness, yes. Some things don't.'

'I mean, even one's serious faults?' *Like sitting here talking to you when my only reason for being in your home is that I want to get at your wife?*

'Certainly,' said Cowley firmly. 'The evil spots in your nature help you to see the truth about evil.'

George Links tried in silence to feed this answer into his mind. It was not in any way esoteric or hard to reconcile with what he knew already, but somehow his mind would not take it. The truth about evil! What did he want to know *that* for? It was, up to now, the one thing he felt conscious of: evil was the element he lived in, deception, equivocation, a toilsome search for pleasure that was, at bottom, self-regarding and even narcissistic.

'Mind you,' Cowley corrected himself, 'when I say the truth about evil, I don't mean to give the word a capital E. I don't mean to speak as if I thought there was such a thing as Evil, a disembodied absolute capable of existing on its own.'

'Don't you think so?' said George Links, with a sudden flash of interest. 'I must say I'm inclined to think there is.'

'Do you believe there's such a thing as heat,' Cowley asked, 'capable of existing apart from the presence of a hot thing?'

'No . . . and yet one can speak of heat as something we recognize wherever we meet it. A hot bowl of soup and a hot July day are both quite different, and yet they both have heat — it's something we can abstract and talk about.'

'That's just it,' said Cowley, spreading one large palm; it was the nearest he seemed able to come to an argumentative gesture. 'The quality, the identity of the heat in a bowl of soup and in a summer afternoon is so different that we've done no more than indicate them both very crudely when we've called them both by that word, *heat*. In just the same way, you can, if you like——'

The kitchen door opened and Ruth came in, wearing a dressing-gown. She had evidently brushed her hair, but the slightly puffy state of the skin round her eyes suggested that she had not yet washed her face. The warmth and indolence of the bed hung about her like a fragrance.

'— crudely indicate evil,' Edward Cowley finished. 'Hullo, darling,' he added. 'Some more tea? It's still quite fresh.'

Ruth sat down in a basket chair near the stove, away from the two men, as if she were aware of carrying with her so much of the ambience of bed that it would not be proper to approach them. George Links, quickly making this analysis, bitterly gave it his approval.

'I'd love some tea,' she said, 'but are you sure it's really fresh? Wouldn't you like to spoil me and make a fresh pot?'

'Well, I can easily do that, of course,' said Cowley. Rising, he took the teapot and went out of the back door, perhaps to empty the leaves out in the place where he had taken the ashes.

Left alone with Ruth, George Links sat paralysed at the table. He had nothing to say, and no means of moving in any direction, mental or physical. For her part, she sat as if alone, seeming unconscious of any pressures in the atmosphere.

Edward Cowley was absent for about twenty-five seconds. For the first ten, George Links sat with nothing perceptible inside him except a sense of desperation. During the second ten, his paralysis slowly ebbed away and was replaced by lust. He dared not turn his head in Ruth's direction — it seemed, to his fevered mind, that the slightest muscular movement would bring some nameless disaster down upon him — but a mordant heat spread evenly through his body until he became aware that his whole being was pounding and blazing. In the midst of this second phase, his mind was gripped by an obsession. He remembered, without having to look at her afresh, that Ruth was wearing pyjamas. He had seen the ends of the trousers beneath her dressing-gown as she walked in.

Suddenly it became the most important question in the world: *Did she wear them always or only in winter?*

The twentieth second ticked away. Steeped in his torturing element, George Links sat as still as ever. But, by degrees, he felt a new sensation: a kind of magnetic pulling at his head, drawing it slowly round towards where Ruth sat.

His head came round. He faced her. She was looking at him.

It was not a long glance; the five remaining seconds easily sufficed to contain it. But not the rest of his life would suffice to get it out of his veins. With a mad, silent gulp, George Links pushed his chair back; then, hearing Cowley's footsteps at the back door, he stumbled out of the room, seized his bag and mackintosh, and was out of the front door. The slam, that was to have been his signal of release, echoed fruitlessly through the house.

.   .   .   .   .

At half-past two he walked up the path, through that garden which, so unguidedly fecund when he first saw it, had now been cowed by the frost into something like orderliness. He rang the bell, wondering what he would say when Ruth came to the door.

But there was no need to say anything. Even as he saw her, through the leaded panes, coming towards the door, he was struck by the almost inhuman purposefulness of her movements. The glass concealed everything except the outline of her shape, but he knew, before seeing it, what the expression on her face would be.

She opened the door and stood back silently. He

entered; without speaking, or looking directly at him, she pushed the door shut, took his hand and began to lead him up the stairs.

One flight, two flights. They were going to the attic, like last time. The attic to which he had said good-bye, only that morning. No wonder it hadn't listened.

They were in the attic, and there was his unmade bed. The door was shut behind them, and still she had not spoken.

'Ruth——'

'Be quiet.'

'But don't you want to know——'

'*Know?*' She brought the word out saturated with bitterness. 'I don't want to know anything. It's too late to know things.'

'All right, then,' he said, taking her grimly by the shoulders. 'We'll have some action.'

'Yes, action, yes, only don't talk. Don't say anything. I hate you when you talk.'

Go on hating me like this, that's all, go on for ever hating me like this.

★ IX ★

CAPTAX moved briskly about his flat, tidying up. His original impulse had been to try to make the place look like a consulting-room, but after the first minute or two this object had been lost in the more general one of simply putting it to rights a bit, making it a more fitting place to entertain a lady. His light, rapid strides, and the eagerness of his movements, betrayed the happiness he was feeling, and gradually he became aware of this.

Happy? Well, why shouldn't he be? Didn't all the signs indicate that a man-sized slap of luck was about to drop into his lap? Here she was, this delightful girl, Janet Links, whom he had looked forward to seeing in his capacity of phoney analyst and making a careful, step-by-step attempt to bring into the net. And here she was, ringing him up in what sounded like agitation, asking for a consultation sooner than they had originally fixed it, saying that she wanted to consult him urgently about something.

'She wants to consult me, she wants to consult me,' Captax hummed to the tune of 'When you wore a tulip'. It certainly was a bound up the ladder. He must have inspired real confidence in her, in that short and interrupted conversation. At this rate, it shouldn't be long before he had the bell ringing in good earnest.

At the same time, he admitted to himself as he bundled an armful of old newspapers out of sight under the bookcase, there was another side to his feelings about the matter. An altruistic, kindly, fatherly side. He was glad that Janet Links felt able to confide in him. He genuinely looked forward to trying to help her. Because, after all, she was a sweet girl. Yes, she really was a very sweet girl.

She was due at three o'clock. Captax glanced at his watch; it was five to three. At the same instant the door-bell shrilled.

Drat! Some pestering fool, coming to clutter up the scene just when he wanted it all nicely cleared for Janet! Captax marched grimly to the door. This pest, whoever he or she was, must be got rid of. The person simply did not exist who could be allowed to butt in just at that moment. It was a time for ruthlessness.

Scowling, he opened the door. It was Janet.

That she should be five minutes ahead of time was already something unlooked for; but his first reaction of mild surprise was immediately engulfed by a second one of real shock, as a small wave, almost touching the shore, is overtaken by a large one. He was shocked, genuinely shaken into self-forgetfulness, by the change in Janet's appearance.

Previously, the chief impression she had made on him had been of daintiness and self-possession. That neat dark head, that elegantly shaped little face with its high cheekbones, topped a trim, spruce figure which she knew how to hold and move without untidiness. Even the absurd upswept frames of her glasses could add nothing more damaging to the *ensemble* than a slight dash of the ludicrous.

That daintiness, as his first glance told him, was now eclipsed. Janet's cheeks seemed to have sunk inwards, leaving her cheekbones jutting out awkwardly. Her whole face seemed to have grown smaller, and this made her eyes stand out unnaturally, so that they were the first thing one noticed. As they were red-rimmed, with an area of dark purple surrounding the red, this made the first impression piteously woebegone. The dulled eyes themselves, blinking out from within their circles of red and purple, unmistakeably told of copious and protracted weeping. They peered at Captax, through those jauntily-framed lenses, with a mute, irresistible appeal.

'What's the matter?' Captax demanded, standing back for Janet to enter. She did so without ceremony, walking past him and straight into the sitting-room as if she did not trust herself to speak.

He shut the door and followed her. Once in the room, she turned to face him, and he noticed, with a fresh wave of astonished indignation, that all her neatness had deserted her. She was wearing a raincoat, buttoned wrongly so that it was all bunched up on one side. Her shoes, which needed polishing, did not match her dress. Who had done this to her?

Captax, for all his man-of-the-world pretensions and his scientific cynicism, was normally rather timid with women. He did not kiss them, for example, unless they showed unmistakeable signs of wanting him to. But he now acted out of character. Although Janet had shown no such signs, he took her in his arms and began to kiss her cheeks and forehead.

Not immediately, but still fairly soon, she put her palms on his chest and gently pushed him away.

'No — no,' she murmured.

'Why not?' Captax demanded; he was suddenly aware that it all mattered to him, mattered terribly.

'Because.'

'Because *what?*'

'Because . . . it's too conventional.'

'I don't see what's conventional about it,' he said, thinking of the odd tangled chain of events that had led to her being here at all. This reminded him of his own assumed identity, which he had momentarily forgotten, and he shook his head in angry bewilderment.

'Oh,' she said impatiently, sitting down, 'it's just one of those situations that are built up on clichés. The errant husband, the tearful little wife, the understanding male friend. He gives her a consoling kiss. Then — pouf!'

'What do you mean, pouf?' asked Captax with interest.

But she had broken off and was staring at him grimly.

'Of course, I forgot,' she said. 'You're not the understanding male friend. You may be grooming yourself for the rôle, but at the moment you're still playing your earlier one.'

Captax, assuming a dignified expression, opened his mouth to say something about his rôle being that of her husband's psycho-analyst. But he closed it again without speaking. It was all so unutterably damned silly.

'Your earlier rôle,' she persisted, blinking at him severely with her tired, tear-quenched eyes. 'The gay bachelor friend of the husband's, who assists him in a little innocent deception. Only it wasn't innocent, and now it isn't even deception.'

Captax, unable to meet her gaze, turned aside and began to walk up and down the room with short, jerky steps. He felt horribly ashamed of himself; it was a most unpleasant sensation, and to combat it he began bringing up all the counter-arguments he could think of. Addressing them not to Janet but to his own conscience, he stumped up and down the carpet in silence, gesturing. *Why* hadn't the deception been innocent? (And why, for that matter, had it stopped being a deception?) He had accepted, without a moment's hesitation, his part in the plot; as if it were axiomatic, not needing any proof, that a husband ought to be helped to hoodwink his wife now and then. *Well, wasn't it?* Didn't all marriages work better if they left room for a certain amount of side-play? He had always vaguely supposed so. But this one didn't seem to have benefited. But again, did it matter much? Was that particular marriage worth saving? Wouldn't this girl be much better off with someone else — someone like himself, for instance?

Janet was sitting back in the armchair, in a more relaxed position than might have been expected, in view of her agitation when she entered the flat. Captax, making one of his turns, caught her eye, and noticed that she was wearing a half-formed smile; its effect was like that of the sun pushing its way through a knot of clouds.

'You are *funny*,' she said appreciatively, as if his appearance and actions, the flat, the furniture, everything, were deliberately contrived in an effort to amuse her. 'The way you go walking up and down moving your hands and talking to yourself.'

'I was *not* talking to myself,' Captax snapped.

'Of course you were.'

'My lips were not moving.'

'Well, you were absolutely wrapped up in your——'

'*Were my lips moving?*'

'No,' she admitted.

'Well, then.'

Tiring of this topic, she introduced the next, as casually as if they were both of the same importance. 'You know, George has been absolutely unscrupulous, the way he's been lying to me.'

Captax gestured as if shaking moisture from his fingers. 'He probably didn't mean you any harm.'

'He didn't mean *me* anything. He was thinking entirely about himself.'

Captax sat down, in the hard chair he used when writing at his desk. 'Well, look at it this way. He was thinking of himself, not minding about you one way or the other. But can you honestly say it made him *treat* you any worse?'

He was proud of the reasonableness of this question. And all the more surprised at its effect, which was to make her burst into tears.

'What's the matter . . . please, please?' he begged, kneeling beside her and putting his arms round her heaving shoulders.

'That's just it — that's just it,' he heard, between sobs.

'What is? *Tell me*,' he urged.

'Oh, God, that's just it,' she wailed, going off into a fresh paroxysm. Captax tried to draw her towards him, to cradle her head against his chest, which was filled with pity for her as if with a tangible unbalance. But the arm of the chair was terribly in the way. She pressed her face into the cushion, snorting, sobbing, whiffling and generally making all the undignified noises women make when they are too stricken by grief to care for appearances. And he knew that he loved her.

At last she stopped, quite abruptly, and sat up straight. Her glasses had fallen off; picking them up, she held them in her hand while she talked, looking myopically into Captax's face.

'That's what made it so cruel. For years George never seemed to take any direct notice of me — he just seemed to accept me as part of the setting of his life, like his job, or the house and garden. And then all of a sudden he seemed to become aware of me as a woman — the change was so spectacular, I suppose I ought to have realized there was something behind it.'

Captax took her hand; she neither resisted nor actively co-operated, but simply let it lie confidingly in his, and went on: 'I just thought it was the result of his beginning to get straightened out by this man he was going to — only of course he wasn't going to any man.'

'I'm sorry about that,' said Captax, as gently as he could.

'It doesn't matter. You didn't know me. I was just a figure off-stage somewhere. Besides, I know men always hang together.'

'But then,' Captax said musingly, beginning to work on the problem, 'this escapade of George's — it really did do something for him, didn't it? It must have given some kind of sense of well-being and confidence, and as a result he was nicer to you. So wasn't it . . .' His voice trailed away.

'I can't deny it,' she said, staring straight ahead. 'The logic of it *is* just that. I did benefit by being tricked. Only now it's impossible, because I know about it.'

They were silent for a moment, then he asked, 'Did you just find out, or did someone tell you?'

'Someone told me. A rather pathetic little man called Evan something.'

'Evan Bone!' shouted Captax, jumping up. 'But surely he didn't——'

'No, he didn't tell me it was his wife that George was carrying on with. It seems he *had* been under that impression, but there'd been some kind of terrific show-down and he'd had it all out with his wife.'

'I can just imagine it,' said Captax, nodding grimly. 'So he starts ranting at her until she gets frightened, or more probably just tired of it all, and to get him to stop barking up the wrong tree she tells him the whole story of what George is really doing.'

'Which she'd learnt from you.'

'Which she'd learnt from me, the little fool. The little bloody fool,' Captax repeated savagely

'Why are you so bitter about her?' Janet asked.

He stopped his pacing of the carpet, and stared at her uncomprehendingly.

'D'you really want to know?'

Janet sat back in her chair. A more relaxed look had come over her face. 'Of course I do. It's always cheering-up to hear about other people's silly mistakes and embarrassments. But there's something I want more, much more.'

Captax stood poised on his short legs, looking thoughtfully at her. 'Let me guess,' he said. 'It can't be a drink, because it's not yet four o'clock in the afternoon.'

'It *is* a drink,' she said. 'A good stiffly mixed drink. I'll accept it in place of the consultation you were going to give me.'

At the word 'consultation' Captax began shame-facedly moving off to the kitchen to fetch glasses. He avoided Janet's eyes; it was painful to be reminded of how he had involved himself in the process of cheating her.

But before he got to the door an impulse of curiosity made him turn round. Janet was looking at him with a new expression; not merely relaxed, but impish — yes, actually *gay*. Nonplussed, he looked away again, then back at her in time to see her tightening her mouth to suppress a smile. He did the same; she made a slight puffing sound; the next moment the dingy room was flooded with the sound of their laughter.

Captax rocked to and fro, guffawing; Janet, he noticed, laughed in a rather unfeminine way, throwing her head back and opening her mouth wide, but the effect was not by any means unattractive. Wiping his eyes, he moved on into the kitchen, put two glasses and some bottles on a tray, and came back to where she sat.

'Gin or whisky?' he asked, and approved of her saying 'Whisky'.

In fact, Captax realized as they clinked glasses and drank, he approved of Janet more every minute. His earlier preoccupation with her had been, largely, sportsmanlike; the wish to add another specimen — howbeit an unusually good one — to the bag. But now he felt as if his narrower intentions were not so much replaced as engulfed by an overwhelming sensation of sheer *approval*; there was no other word. She was a real top-notcher. She was all right. Good all the way through. His mind clumsily groped for phrases.

'More cheerful now?' he asked her.

She nodded. 'Though I don't at all see why I should be. None of my problems are solved.'

He said quickly, to head off any melancholy reflections, 'Oh — don't let's talk about your problems. Let's talk about mine instead.'

Immediately he regretted this: he felt unable to withstand the sort of scrutiny she would doubtless give him. Sure enough, she set her glass down and began looking at him intently.

'Your problems must be quite knotty ones,' she said. 'You seem to be mixed up in half-a-dozen plots at once.'

Nettled, he suddenly broke in, 'That's not fair, damn it. You make me sound like the sort of person who *enjoys* plotting and scheming. In fact any bachelor whose friends are mostly married gets into this kind of scrape very easily, out of sheer good-nature. These married bastards always assume that they can count on a single man to help them when they want to break out now and then.'

He refilled her glass, and they both sat silent, immersed in their own thoughts. Janet spoke next.

'Why is it?' she asked simply. 'Why do they want to deceive us?'

Captax shrugged. 'I've only seen it from the outside. But I'd say that they didn't want to deceive you, as a primary object. I mean that there's no particular pleasure in the deception. If a husband wants to run after another woman, he accepts it as an unpleasant necessity that he'll have to tell lies to his wife. He doesn't *enjoy* it, however skilfully he brings it off.'

'Do you think George hated having to lie to me?'

The question came abruptly, almost crudely. Captax felt helpless and resentful. How should *he* know what George's feelings had been? And yet he did know. George had simply not cared one way or the other, provided he could get what he was out for. It would be too cruel to tell Janet that, in just those words. All right, he could start telling lies again: tell her that George had suffered, had been dragged out of shape by conflicting emotions.

And make her want to go back to George again?

'Why don't you speak?' she asked.

'Because I haven't anything to say that you'd care to hear.'

She bent her head so that her cheek lay in her open palm: a gesture of helplessness, as if her neck had lost the will to hold up her head.

'I know. George didn't love me, did he?'

'No,' said Captax flatly.

For an instant he thought she would collapse into another vortex of grief and pain: but though her face was hidden from him, he knew instinctively that the shadow that travelled across it was gone as quickly as it came.

All this time she had been holding her glasses limply in her left hand. Now, suddenly straightening up, she put them on and looked at him squarely. He understood; it was the equivalent of girding one's loins.

'Don't go,' he cried anxiously.

'I wasn't going.'

'Oh,' he subsided. 'It's just that with your glasses on you look — prepared for movement, somehow.'

'I am prepared for movement,' she said levelly.

Captax looked up at her, trying to gauge her mood. 'What kind of movement?'

'Any kind. I can't go on staying where I am. Everyone else has moved, now I'm going to.'

'You mean' — he hesitated — 'move *physically*? Stop living with George?'

'Probably,' she said in the same matter-of-fact tone. 'But not necessarily at once. There are more important moves than physical ones, and some of those I've already made.'

Captax stood up. His pulse was thundering in his ears. Nothing, he now understood, had ever happened to him before this moment.

'Take one thing into account,' he croaked, his voice skidding through his dry throat, 'when you plan these moves of yours.'

'What thing?'

'I love you,' he said.

For a long time he stood motionless. Then, seeing that she was not going to speak, he picked up the tray and carried it out into the kitchen. There, he put the tray down on the draining-board, turned on the hot tap, and ran some water into the washing-up bowl. When the bowl was full of water of a suitable temperature, he shook some soap powder into it. Next he put the two glasses into the water, and, taking the sponge rubber mop in his right hand, carefully washed them, concluding by rinsing them under the cold tap. Finally he poured the hot soapy water away, squeezed out the sponge rubber mop under the tap and left the sink tidy.

Only he forgot to turn off the cold tap, and it ran and ran, wasting gallons of water, and there was no time to turn it off because Janet had stumbled into the kitchen and was in his arms.

★ X ★

GEORGE LINKS was too buoyant with happiness to stand still on the escalator. Swinging his brief-case delightedly, he swarmed up the steps two at a time, thus obtaining an intoxicating impression of speed. From time to time (for the escalators at the Paddington Tube Station are used by many people who have an insufficient grasp of the usages of city life) he had to pause while a clot of passengers reluctantly regrouped into single file to let him pass; but he never failed to reward and mollify these voyagers with a charming smile.

The smile was not forced; it was part of his entirely genuine well-being. So this was happiness! He had never, so far as he could remember, experienced anything like it in his life before. Of course there must have been times when he had been happy as a child; but when he searched his memory of childhood for deposits of pure happiness, he could only find things like Christmas Eve — times when his whole body had been suffused with an emotion that could, from some points of view, be called happiness; but from others it was almost torture. There was too much excitement, too much painful agitation, in that childish happiness; what he was feeling now was more settled, fulfilled, secure of itself. He felt, what no child has ever felt, that his happiness had come into his life as a solidly established ingredient. No sudden reverse of fate could obliterate it all in a moment. Even — George Links reflected, reaching the top of the escalator and synchronising his muscular movements with the speed of the apparatus — if Ruth were to ditch him now, even *that* would not plunge him into immediate wretchedness. He would suffer, yes, and the suffering would mount up until it reached the pitch where he was really wretched; but for a long time there would be a glow in his life, similar to the glow of a gas-fire after being turned off.

But what was he doing, thinking in those terms? Why on earth *should* Ruth ditch him? Surely she was in the bag for a long time now. As evidences of Ruth's being in the bag crowded in upon his mind, George Links became dreamy-eyed and moved forward somnambulistically. Arriving at the London Transport barrier, he gave up his Western Region ticket, and had walked some yards before the skirling of the ticket-collector penetrated his ears. Returning, he put down his bag, accepted the return of his Western Region ticket, put it in a safe pocket, and began searching his clothing for his London Transport ticket. He was not wearing a waistcoat, so the number of his pockets was, at the moment, rather small: only nine, counting the two in his overcoat. It was the work of a moment to turn out all nine, and the work of another moment to rearrange the contents and turn them out again; but no ticket came to light. No London Transport ticket, that is. It was his Western Region ticket that seemed always to be emerging from the recesses of various linings to greet with a coy capitulation the rapturous embrace of his fingers.

During the whole performance George Links's good humour did not desert him. It remained firmly in place, and so did his indulgent smile and the dreamy look in his eyes. A miracle worked by happiness! He felt it, the ticket-collector felt it, and most of the stream of people who went past them were aware of it in one way or another.

Janet was aware of it. She had, unwittingly, set foot on the bottom step of the escalator at the moment when George Links had quitted the top one; quite by chance — the world is full of these chances — her timing had been as perfect as if she had intended it as a gesture, to indicate that there could not be room, on the same upward-gliding spool, for the two of them.

Now, as George Links scooped out his right-hand hip pocket for the fourth time, extracting from it with an immediately quenched exclamation of triumph the Western Region ticket he would have sworn to having put back, a moment before, in his breast pocket, Janet walked past him. Pausing within twelve inches of his back, she handed her London Transport ticket to the collector, and went on her way to the Western Region station.

Was there the faintest suggestion of an additional pause, a slight hesitancy which spilled over into the time after she had safely handed over her ticket? Did the muscles of her body, accustomed for a thousand nights to guiding themselves towards George Links in the warm cocoon of the bedclothes, flutter for a second in his direction, confessing to an impulse to distract his

attention from the quest for the fascinating card-
board? If so, the tremor never reached her bones. She
saw him; her cool glance took in the entire situation;
she could even, had she wished, have reminded him
that it was his habit, when sitting with crossed legs on
the longitudinal benches of an underground train, to
slip his ticket into the turn-up of his more accessible
trouser leg — where in fact it lay at the moment,
advertising its presence only by the protrusion of one
modest green corner.

Did nothing stir in her? If, incredibly, her mating
instinct was dormant, was there no impulse from her
wifely instinct? Perhaps there was; perhaps a bystander
who happened at that moment to be within a few
feet of Janet would have heard a curiously dry, painful
click: the dislocation of an instinct. For surely there was
a mechanism that swung into action there, sending up
to the brain a murmur, never uttered, of 'The turn-up,
darling?'

At all events, George Links missed the train, and
Janet, settled comfortably in a non-smoker, was already
a quarter of a mile along the route towards home when
he, with several dents in that shining good humour,
surged up to the barrier.

.   .   .   .   .

An hour later the next train left, this time duly
bearing George Links. His equanimity had, on the
whole, borne up well. Missed the train? Never mind,
take the next. The next would be more crowded with
country people returning from their evening out?
Then travel First Class and pay the excess.

Accordingly, then, George Links sat in unaccustomed

comfort, blinking through the dark window at the lights of Paddington, of Southall, of Ealing. The train smoothly gathered pace; he stretched out his feet luxuriously; his muscles were at ease. For the first time since he had taken leave of Ruth, about two hours previously, he could relax physically and let his body slide into the same state of opulent satiety in which his mind was already steeped.

The train swayed rhythmically. The cushions were soft, his head was pillowed. Ruth, Ruth! The other passengers seemed to have wined and dined well; they glanced somnolently at newspapers or slumbered outright. George Links sank back and let the physical memory of that afternoon glow along his skin, permeate his muscles, light up his bones.

But.

But what? It had all happened, it was true, it was only a couple of hours since he had left her, he was going back again next week, they had really said and done all those things:

But.

George Links shifted irritably as if the seat were uncomfortable; a notable slander on British Railways. He stared vacantly out of the window, then shut his eyes, deliberately flooding his mind with images of Ruth, her complaisance, her audacities, her silences. For a moment he was engulfed, but this time the flood receded with unmistakable sharpness. Something *was* wrong.

The ticket-collector came in and George Links had to feel in his pockets for silver, then wait while the man laboriously made out a chit authorizing the social trespass. Again he twisted uneasily on the cushions, trying to evade the sharp thoughts that were beginning to prod into him. The ticket-collector, having seen economic justice done, withdrew, shutting the door. There were no more diversions. He had to face it.

Face what? The fact that his pleasure was ebbing away and leaving in its place a cruel, rocky shore of pain. He tried once more to cling to the pleasure, the opulence, the comfort, but it slid through his hands like retreating liquid.

God damn it! Abruptly, George Links stood up, opened the door and went out into the corridor, leaving the expensive comfort he had paid for, to stare grimly out at the dark frozen landscape. Might as well face it. He knew what was wrong. It was the knowledge that Ruth did not belong to him, that in her life he could never occupy more than a corner.

That was all. There was no point in agonizing over it. Just a simple fact that had to be faced. It was always going to be like this, always, always. It was nobody's fault; he had started out in that particular direction, had even, initially, congratulated himself on the fact that she had a husband, nicely taking care of all the material responsibility.

All right, let it go. There was nothing he could do about it. Better not to be under any illusions. Better to know, clear-sightedly, just how much and how little he counted for in Ruth's scheme of things. He was her diversion. A little fun that she needed, to help her through a dry patch in her life. There was no escape, in any direction. It was useless, for instance, to try to swamp the situation in sheer physical pleasure. The unreflecting glow could be produced, infallibly —

he had just seen that — but, just as infallibly, it drained away. And it was equally useless to imagine that, if the torment became too much, he could break away. Sooner or later, when Ruth no longer needed him, she would ditch him: that would be that, and there was no point in trying to fool himself that he would have the strength to anticipate her decision, even by one day, even if it were a question of saving the very foundations of his pride.

The pounding of the train became noticeably slower. They were arriving at the first stop, where he would get out and travel the rest of the way by a branch line. *A branch line!* — perhaps that was the solution. Many a life had been saved, he reflected — or, if not saved, rendered liveable — by the successful grouping of secondary endeavours round principal endeavours that were fatally split.

The train drummed slowly in to the platform and halted. George Links went back into the compartment for his case, took it down, and got out. There, waiting in its accustomed bay, was the local train. His own train, less impressive than the shrieking, thundering express, but personal, accommodating, tailored to his own needs.

He got in, and stood once more in the corridor, watching the silent fields as the engine creakingly drew forward. The thought of Ruth, the memory of her bounty, the agony of her separateness, seemed mercifully dulled; held off, as it were, by a protective fence. He was going home. Janet would be at home. Within an hour or so of his arrival, it would be time for bed. Bed with Janet in it! — how had he ever mis-prized such a combination? How could he have felt such discontent, such rebellious promptings to go outside and expose himself to the lacerations of illicit love?

Well, but he had. It was done, and it was too late to go back on it. Ruth had him fast. But Janet, thank God, had him fast too. She was the perfect refuge from the furies that Ruth had set in pursuit of him. She had the one thing Ruth lacked most signally: gentleness. But then — and the thought came as a great twist of the knife in his vitals — Ruth probably *did* have gentleness in her. All women had. It was just that she was not in a position to bestow it on him. She had, after all, her own defences to keep up. That was something it had taken him this long to learn. A woman can give her fierceness to a man and still be intact; if she gives him her gentleness, he has won her.

The train chuffed round a curve. The lights of his town winked out. Janet was there, waiting for him: she who had given him her gentleness. Standing motionless in the corridor, George Links searched in his dry heart for the strength to abjure Ruth, to leave her alone for ever, to come back to Janet and take root in her gentleness. He could not find it. Ruth must go when she chose; he could not choose it. Next he searched for crumbs of guilt about Janet. After all, it was inhuman — wasn't it? — to use a fellow human being as an accessory, an implement, something whose rôle was dictated by circumstances.

But he could find no guilt. All he knew, as he got out of the train and began to hurry towards the station exit, was that he needed Janet's gentleness as he had never needed it during all the years she had lavished

it on him — that at last, in a word, he appreciated
her.

.   .   .   .   .

The front door closed behind him. The hall light
was on, but all the downstairs rooms were dark. He
peeped into the sitting-room; the fire was almost
burnt out, though the room was warm, as if Janet had
been sitting there beside a good blaze for an hour or
two. A pang ran through him. She had been sitting
here, in the home they had made for themselves; and
what had he been doing?

He went back into the hall and called, 'Janet?'

There was no answer, so, slipping off his outdoor
shoes from force of habit, he went on up the stairs. The
bedroom door was closed, and, when he opened it,
darkness confronted him.

'Janet?' he asked urgently. Her shape was humped
under the bedclothes.

'Mm?'

'Aren't you feeling well, darling?'

There was a short but perceptible pause before she
answered, 'I'm all right.'

'Well, you won't mind if I put the light on, then,
will you?'

She made no answer. He touched the switch of the
least powerful light they had in the room; darkness
gave place to a soft twilight.

George Links stood expectantly, his stockinged
feet aware of the thick bedroom rug. But Janet made
no move. Neither turning to look at him nor shrink-
ing more deeply into the bedclothes, she lay as if
the light had not been turned on, as if he were not
there.

Irresolute, he paused, then asked again, 'Sure you're all right, darling?'

'I've made you a bed in the spare room,' she said suddenly.

George Links's hand went mechanically to his tie and began unfastening it. The rest of his body was frozen, shocked into uncomprehending stone, but for some reason that hand went on moving, ineffectually, not joined by the other.

He plucked at his tie a few times and then said, 'You've done what?'

She did not repeat her words. The light glowed on, she lay still in her own half of the bed, and George Links's feet sank deeply into the bedroom rug as if it were the Slough of Despond.

Then, switching off the light, he moved uncomprehendingly, shifting his limbs with a curiously inhuman deliberation, as if he had only just worked out the theory of how to walk and was freshly engaged in putting it into practice. Only when he saw the neat, cold little bed awaiting him, with a clean towel lying across one corner, did he realize, tearingly, what he had become: in his own house, a politely tolerated guest.

. . . . .

George Links lived out the next six days within a dry vacuum. In the cold logic of his insanity, he knew that his contact with reality had been snapped, and that he could only wait for the tide of events to drift him back into some kind of meaningful relationship with the world. 'Drift' was the right word, for he and Janet had suddenly become two icebergs; on the evening of the first day, he clumsily tried to provoke an air-clearing thunderstorm, broaching the subject from the end of his banishment from the bedroom; but he could not, even at that point, bring himself to a complete display of candour, and did not say — was not even momentarily impelled to say — anything about Ruth. As a result, he had felt the falsity of his protests, and knew that Janet felt it too and despised him for it; she answered with a short, concisely phrased refusal to 'discuss the whole business'.

The days went by at a curiously regular pace. Though hellish, they did not, curiously, seem longer than usual. He simply attacked them with cold malice, like a man breaking up flagstones, and somehow put them behind him one by one. And all the time his eye was steadily fixed on the day when he had next arranged to see Ruth. This time, all evasion was to be over. Janet was simply not available for the rôle of second-string comforter. She had renounced it. Perhaps, if he withdrew his emotions from Ruth and turned them in full force towards Janet, he would be able to bring her round, given time. But this was not, in practical terms, an idea that could be considered. The plain fact was, he *could not* withdraw his emotions from Ruth, either wholly or partly. She had him, fast. And since there was no comfort along the stony road he had been treading, the way ahead was clearly marked out. He had to get Ruth to leave Cowley and come to him. The divorce, or rather the double divorce, would follow at its own pace. If he could get Ruth to agree to it, the rest would be easy. *If?* — he *had* to get her to.

It was the week before Christmas, and George Links

could not help but be aware that the thunderous surf of the festive season was beating against the household and being stormily repulsed, as by a lighthouse. Christmas cards dropped through the letter-box at intervals increasingly short and decreasingly predictable. Janet always gathered them up from the mat, and always, after a perfunctory glance at the signatures, put them in a neat pile on top of the bookcase in the living-room. The pile grew and grew, and tragic discontent radiated from it. Janet's refusal to stand the cards up where they could be seen, the flat and uncompromising way she laid them tidily on top of one another, expressed more clearly than words that she had given up caring. She had completely withdrawn her emotions from the home they had built up: George Links understood this, and, with a dry pang that went too deep to be felt as ordinary suffering, he accepted it. The Christmas cards lay on their sides, one above the other, like kind words locked away where they could never be heard.

Nevertheless, the only times, during that week, when George Links felt that his calm was in danger were the moments when he was racked by the wild impulse to hurry off at once to London, irrupt into the Cowley household, and plunge the drama there and then into its last scene. But these fits never lasted long. Deeply, he knew that this period of waiting, of forcing himself to let the pre-arranged time come round, was a necessary preliminary discipline. The task was not, in any case, going to be easy; by rushing into it in a dishevelled way, giving the impression that he was acting from nerve-sick impulsiveness rather than cast-iron, manly resolve, he would only make it ten times harder.

Manly resolve! Cast-iron! His veins seemed to empty of blood and fill with a hard, flinty dust, which shifted about like powder as he walked, and, when he lay down at night, poured sluggishly into his head. In this state, the days went by. Even Sunday, with no office to go to, passed somehow. And then it was the day, and he was at the local station, then the main station, then, then, then, then, then, London.

Christmas was now only five days away, and as soon as he stepped off the train George Links felt himself swirled away in a current of blowsy Yuletide gaiety. There was a Christmas tree with coloured lights winking palely in the murk of the station; everywhere, people scurried about with parcels; the endless scribble of advertising, which covered London from ground-level to the top of the highest building and stretched away to every horizon, had taken on a new stridency in its coaxing and bullying. 'Get your fuel — your wine — your food — your drugs — your gramophone records — your cigarettes — your mountain of para-phernalia *for Christmas!*' they screamed everywhere, as if Christmas was a day of reckoning on which everyone's locker was to be searched, and those found without all these goods flogged unmercifully. True enough, George Links thought. He picked his way along the littered pavement, wanly staring about him, feeling like a ghost. Christmas! It was part of the world of everyday reality from which he was excluded, and which he must remain outside of until Ruth turned the key and admitted him.

And after that? He shrugged as the thought occurred to him. What could anything else matter? His divorce

might raise certain professional difficulties, but what
the hell. Any business firm could use a man with a
knowledge of the law, even if he found it, for a time,
difficult to go on practising as a solicitor. And in any
case, he could not think of it, could not see it as a real
problem, until he had Ruth there. When he could see,
hear and touch her, get her opinion on it all, he would
feel that the situation had normal reality. Until then,
all was fantasy; and the enormous selling bonanza that
was going on about him, in its astonishing flood of
genuine goodwill, even a grain here and there of genuine
piety, with unscrupulous salesman's razzmatazz, height-
ened his sense of living in a dream.

He got on to a bus, and sank back with a sigh as it
crawled along. Ruth had agreed to meet him at a pub
they both knew; not the regular one in which he met
Captax, but a well-known landmark of a place in the
middle of the area where she would be doing her
Christmas shopping. Would she be getting him anything? He pictured her coming in, wrapped in overcoat and scarf, with a basket of parcels done up in gay
paper. Would she, on greeting him, take out one of
the smaller parcels and hand it to him? 'Darling
George — it's not a real present, but . . . just to show
I've been thinking of you.' The paper with its gay holly
pattern comes away with a crackle: a tube of shaving
cream, a bar of chocolate, a cigar: 'But how sweet
of you!' How happy she could make him, and so
easily.

The bus went past the pub, too fast for him to jump
off, and continued for what seemed a quarter of an
hour before pulling up. When it stopped George Links
leapt off and began running. His stoical patience was

breaking up at last. Quickly, quickly! Into the pub, take up your position! The week really *has* gone by, it *is* the day, and now it actually is the hour, almost the very minute. They had agreed on 12.15, and his watch, scrupulously kept on time, showed 12.07.

He went in. The place was about one-third full, but the wild profusion of Christmas decorations would have made it seem crowded without the presence of a single patron. Huge paper streamers fought each other for right of way across the ceiling; bells, clumsily fashioned of the same material, nodded and bobbed everywhere. Above the array of bottles behind the bar, fairy lights had been planted as densely as sequins.

George Links ordered a whisky and sat down. He had specified the saloon bar, and this had only one door that gave on to the street. Through this door, then, Ruth must enter. He sat squarely facing it, determined to see her the very instant she came in. After all, if she were there two or three seconds before he saw her, that would be two or three unnecessary seconds spent on the rack. For it *was* the rack, now that his stoicism had blown away: the rack, the dentist's drill, anything you liked to name. It was here and he was going through it. But courage: courage and calm: it was nearly over. In a moment or two Ruth would appear. He would gather her into his arms, into his life, and everything would begin properly at last.

His glass was empty. The watch, in contemptuous contrast to the pub clock, showed 12.19. She couldn't be long now. It was worth having another drink. Two whiskies was more than he would normally drink while waiting for someone, but this time it was perfectly rational and excusable. He refilled, at the last minute yielding to impulse and ordering a double.

The double lasted him twenty minutes. During that time the impulse to drain his glass at a single gulp attacked him, on a sober estimate, three hundred and fifty times, and each time he successfully beat it off. So who said he was losing his control? His control was iron, granite, case-hardened steel, anything hard you could think of. It was provoking, of course, that Ruth should be late, to-day of all days. But then she was not to know that he had set his heart so much on seeing her on the dot. On the contrary, she probably reasoned that, with the Christmas crowds and the rush of last-minute shopping, he would not mind an unusual disregard, to-day, of normal punctuality.

The whisky was the main trouble. He obviously ought to have another drink; but three — no, it would be four, with the double — four whiskies was rather a lot to have while waiting for someone. Should he change to beer? Never: that would be worse than ever. Must stick to the same.

He decided to give her five minutes, during which he would make no decision, order no drink, and, as far as possible, think no thought. He closed his eyes. Perhaps Ruth would be standing in front of him when he next opened them. In that case, he would be closing his eyes on his old life, opening them on his new one. A splendid thing to do.

Stubbornly, George Links sat on, facing the door, his eyes tight shut. Knowing that the time-sense can play strange tricks, he decided, after sitting for what felt like half an hour, that one minute had probably elapsed. Doggedly, he sat out another half-hour, translating this into another minute. Finally, he opened his eyes.

Ruth was not there. He looked at his watch. He had kept his eyes shut for six minutes and some odd seconds; becoming, in the process, the object of sympathetic glances from his fellow-patrons. As the fact registered itself, his legs began to move. It was an entirely automatic action. He could not be said to have 'decided' to move, to get out of the pub, to go round to the Cowleys'. Quite simply, the end of his endurance had come, and his body began to move of its own accord. As he passed by a corner of the bar he put down his empty whisky glass, without knowing that he did so. The paper bells quivered in the draught as he pulled open the door. A MERRY CHRISTMAS grinned at him once more from above the bar, and he was outside.

A bus came past, going in what was vaguely the right direction, and George Links boarded it; but immediately the dryness and terror of his situation caught him chokingly by the throat. One doesn't, he thought, travel to Golgotha, even a spongy, self-centred little Golgotha, on a bus. One goes there either by the quickest means available, or by the slowest. The bus slowed down at a corner, and George Links stepped off, his mind still working at the metaphor. Golgotha was wrong. What was right? Canossa, perhaps?

A taxi. He hailed it and was inside. A taxi to Canossa. He remembered, however, to give the driver the correct address, and to say 'Swiss Cottage'. The driver nodded impatiently. He knew where to go, just from the name of the road. No need to tell *him* it was Swiss Cottage. George Links sat back on the spruce leather, envying the driver. He was in control.

Disciplined. They had to go round on bicycles. Pedalling about, day after day, getting to know all the streets. Then they were allowed to take out licences. Everything taken care of.

The man's bicycling experience stood him in good stead, and soon they were at the gate of the familiar straggling garden, coins had chinked, and the taxi had gone. George Links felt his legs carry him down the path. He saw his hand rise to the bell. All was automatic. There was no central identity to which it all referred. What, then, took its place? What controlled the central switchboard, keeping the nervous impulses sorted out? An easy one. The whisky. The whisky, bought in the shouting Christmas pub, moved him along, glowing within him like a switched-off soul.

In answer to his ring, Edward Cowley opened the door almost at once. The whisky had not told George Links what to do if it were not Ruth who came to the door, but his tongue seemed able to move without any hesitation.

'I wanted to see Ruth, if she's available.'

Cowley shook his head. It seemed to George Links that he conveyed not refusal, not hostility, but a pure negative. As if he had been asked, 'Is it one o'clock yet?'

'I'm afraid you can't,' he said.

'She's out?' George Links felt the whisky push the syllables out into the air, his tongue, lips and larynx obediently moving.

Cowley looked at him without expression.

'She's out — she's in but she doesn't want to see you — what's the difference?'

'Unless I'm mistaken, there's a lot of difference.'

Cowley looked at George Links meditatively for a second before answering, 'You *are* mistaken.'

Suddenly the whisky drained away from George Links's nervous system, and left him with nothing. He could neither speak nor move. Contradictory impulses began flashing through his disordered network: to turn and go, to force his way into the house, to lie down on his back, to leap at Cowley and attack him. He stood feeling the messages tangle, the confusions pile up.

Then he heard Cowley's voice, addressing him.

'Sorry — what did you say?'

'I said, Come in a minute. We might as well put the thing into words, for your sake anyway.'

What thing?

'Come on in,' said Cowley, holding the door more widely open. He seemed different. Where did the difference lie? Was he more animated? Not exactly; his physical repose seemed just as massive as ever. Leading the way into the kitchen, he sat down on a plain wooden chair, and motioned George Links to sit near the fire, with all his old calmness of movement. And yet there *was* a change. Even in his dispersed conditions, George Links could feel it. Cowley no longer seemed withdrawn. He had come back from whatever planet had been the scene of his exile.

'So Ruth doesn't want to see me?' George Links asked. In an impersonal way, as if he were a spectator of the scene, he sensed that there was no need of any evasion. Whatever there was to know, Cowley knew. It was he, now, who was the questioner.

Cowley brought his large, smooth hands together in his lap. For a moment, as if marshalling his thoughts, he contemplated them. Then he raised his eyes to George Links's face.

'I'm just hoping, for your sake,' he said, 'that you've got the courage, or can find it from somewhere, to take what you're going to have to take without going under. I hope that genuinely. But if you can't, there isn't anything I can do to help you. I'm just not placed so as to be able to.'

George Links felt a stiffening of rebellious pride. Go under? Why should he? Because it was all over with Ruth, as it patently was? Because all the evasions, all the doubling and twisting, were no use any more? To hell with it. It would only be a help, in the long run; it would force him to throw all his energies into recovering Janet.

'Don't worry,' he said. 'Just tell me what you think I ought to know. I'll take care of how to weather it.'

'It isn't any credit to me,' Cowley went on, ignoring him, 'that I don't feel angry with you. I hardly could, in view of the fact that our cases are so similar.'

'*Our* cases? *Similar?*'

Cowley nodded. 'I've only just recovered from something like the same state of disorganization that you're still in. Mine took the form of an intellectual quandary, and to some extent it had intellectual causes, but the differences aren't as important as the resemblances. I wasn't fit to keep my end up in normal human life, any more than you are. My particular kind of disorganization didn't lead me into petty disreputability, as yours has led you, but that's just a difference of temperament. It led me to something worse. After all, it's a peculiar kind of hell to have a wife like Ruth and know that you're not providing her with the kind of love and happiness that she must have.'

George Links opened his mouth to speak, but Cowley went on unheeding. 'It's something you wouldn't understand, because you don't know, yet, what it is to give your whole allegiance to one person. When you do, you'll be able to imagine what real love is, and then you'll also have an inkling of what genuine failure can be.'

George Links said, 'Isn't what I have now — isn't that failure?'

'Objectively, yes,' said Cowley, nodding. 'Seen from the outside, it's failure. But from where you're standing, I don't see how real failure can be envisaged. Because it's only the reverse side of real achievement, and I'm sure you just don't know what that is.'

With an abrupt gesture of impatience, George Links stood up to go. 'If all you can do is to be sententious, I'll be——'

'Just a minute,' Cowley broke in. 'I haven't told you yet what I'm being sententious *about*.'

'No, but you don't need to tell me. It's all perfectly clear to me, imperceptive as you think I am. You've come out of this intellectual quandary you've been in for a good many months. So, among other things, you've rediscovered Ruth as a woman. You also know about the part she's been allowing me to play in her life. Either you've known all along, subconsciously, or she's told you since you re-established contact with her, or — and perhaps this is the most likely — since you found her again you've just realized everything without any need for words. I don't know and I can hardly expect you to tell me. But, in any case, you've been able to make that situation obsolete and now you're telling me it's obsolete. Is that right?'

'It's right,' said Cowley, 'as far as it goes.'

'Well, doesn't it go most of the way?'

Cowley made no answer, and George Links, misinterpreting his silence, went on with a volubility in which there was a hint of triumph. 'I dare say there's a detail here and there I haven't divined, but I should imagine my picture's pretty clear. And since you've been good enough to tell me you don't feel angry with me, I'll return the compliment by telling you, genuinely, that I'm glad you've got things straightened out.'

Cowley looked up at him. 'You're glad,' he said meditatively.

'Yes, I'm glad. You may think me a bit of a worm, but I can be objective enough — at this moment, anyway — to see that it's much better for you and Ruth to be making each other happy than for an awkwardly messy kind of triangle to be in existence.'

'You can see that, can you?' said Cowley in the same meditative tone. 'So you know what it is to care about other people — to be interested in their happiness?'

George Links nodded. 'I do. It's a fairly recent development, I admit — sometime in the last few hours, probably — but I feel I *have* made an advance, and that it isn't just a passing state of mind.'

Cowley sat silent for a moment. Then he looked across at George Links with a curiously appraising look, as if he were a doctor trying to assess how much punishment a man could stand. A prison doctor, perhaps, giving a convict the once-over before authorizing a flogging.

'What's the matter?' George Links asked. Nervousness, a sense of rising alarm, made his tone harsh and abrupt.

Cowley still paused before answering, and drew in his breath rather deeply, as if about to say something that could not afterwards be taken back.

'This new knowledge of yours,' he said, 'this concern for other people, and awareness of what goes on in their minds. I'm glad to hear that you feel you've got a fairly secure hold on it: because it's about the only way of scraping together the courage to withstand one's own misfortunes.'

'It's kind of you to care whether I can stand my own misfortunes.' George Links felt justified in allowing an ironical note to filter into his voice; after all, Cowley had no need to sermonize him so directly.

'I wouldn't utter an opinion one way or the other,' said Cowley, indicating clearly that he had caught the note of ironic reproof. 'Only it so happens that I've got the unpleasant task of telling you a piece of bad news.'

As soon as he heard the words, George Links knew immediately that Janet had left him. There was no need for Cowley to say it explicitly. It had to be that; there was nothing else that could be such a major disaster, nothing that Cowley would feel the need to approach so hesitantly.

'Thank you,' he said, his voice dry as powdered glass. 'It was nice of you to lead up to it so carefully.'

'You know what I was going to . . .?'

'I know my wife must have left me. It's the only thing you'd break to me in this massively gentle way. I don't know how you know, or whether there are any details you have to tell me, but I know that.'

Cowley nodded. 'Some things just communicate themselves, I know. I'm rather relieved you didn't make me put it into words.'

George Links, sitting up erect in his chair, began mentally examining himself to see what was broken, like a person climbing out of a wrecked motor-car. Janet had left him. He knew, now, that he loved Janet and that losing her was worse than losing Ruth, whom he had never rightly or fully possessed. And yet he could speak, frame sentences, think clearly; grief had not stunned him.

'How do you know?' he asked. 'Not that it greatly matters. But presumably Janet somehow got to know that I was involved with Ruth, and chose to inform me through you as a way of getting at all of us together.'

'Not at all,' said Cowley flatly. 'Your wife doesn't come into the picture at all, as far as I've been concerned. She hasn't communicated with either Ruth or me; quite possibly she doesn't know we exist.'

'Then who . . .' George Links meant to frame a coherent question, but suddenly his voice failed to come through. His throat felt as if it were stuffed with felt. This must be the beginning of his reaction to the words uttered a moment ago.

'Do you really want to know?'

He nodded, gripping the wooden arms of his chair. Facts, solid neutral facts, were all that could bring any comfort.

'Well,' said Cowley with a faint shrug, as if obeying a whim, 'it's Captax.'

George Links heard the name, and recognised to whom it applied. But he could attach no real meaning to the information. He had wanted facts, but now that he had a fact it did not penetrate into his consciousness.

It was too late. A minute ago, yes. But now, the grief and shock had spread from his brain and reached the centres where it really mattered.

He tried to speak again. In vain.

Cowley, sitting as immobile as ever, looked up at him. In his eyes George Links read a detached but genuine commiseration.

'You remember,' said Cowley, 'I said I hoped you could find the courage to take a bad knock.'

The felt still obstructed George Links's throat. He stood with his arms hanging limply by his sides, struggling to speak, move, do anything that would break the nightmare. Cowley sat watching him with that curious impersonal pity: ah, there was a man who could help, if he would! George Links felt again the urge to appeal to Cowley, to draw strength from the man's resources, as he had done on the morning when the snakes were thrashing in his chest. But how could he make the appeal? He tried to think, but no words would form. No. No, it was impossible. There were no terms in which such an appeal could ever be framed. No help, no help. He struggled against a wave of panic — then heard Cowley speaking to him, his voice gentle.

'May I give you a piece of advice?'

George Links nodded.

'It's just this. Don't go home. She isn't there, and she won't be coming back. You've lost her and that's all there is to it.'

Home? To the Christmas cards lying on their sides? *But where else was there to go?*

'You'd better go now,' said Cowley, still gently. Rising, he led the way to the front door and opened it. As George Links was obediently shambling out, his eyes like those of a man anaesthetised, Cowley put a hand on his arm and halted him for a moment.

'Don't forget,' he said. 'Don't go home. You'll find your own resources if you can just get over this first shock. But you must get out of your normal routines if you're going to break the worst of the fall. Don't do any of your usual things for a bit.'

George Links nodded. Then, feeling that Cowley might not realize that he was signifying agreement, he shook his head. Cowley released his arm, he moved forward automatically, and the door closed behind him.

But what else was there to do except the usual things? And where else was there to go except the places he had been to before? It was all different, of course, all different, because of Christmas. Nowhere looked quite the same with Christmas roaring and pealing every-where. And none of it could be the same again for another reason. Because of the silence at the heart of Christmas. Because of the tenderness he had mislaid.

George Links walked on. The pavements became more crowded as he went towards the centre of the city. Many of the people had gaily-wrapped parcels under their arms. Darkness began to fall, and the shop windows blazed with the promise of impossible luxuries. Doggedly he walked and walked, his body carrying itself without instructions, like a riderless horse out searching its stable. At last he reached the familiar pub that had been their meeting-place.

The saloon bar was very full, and George Links did not see Captax.

* XI *

CAPTAX ran eagerly up the stone steps, laughing inwardly as he realised that it was the first time for years that he had done anything so energetic: since he became fat, in fact. Before reaching the top he was already diving into his pocket for the key. It was inserted, the door was unlocked and pushed open, he was inside, and with hardly a pause in the rapid rhythm of his footfalls he was in the sitting-room, ready to pull off his overcoat. *Home!* his body sang to itself.

Janet was not to be seen, but a delicious smell of meat and vegetables wafted out from the kitchen, and in a moment she appeared, wearing an apron and looking rather flushed. She had a small black smudge on one side of her face, and her hair was not as smooth as usual. In addition, she had taken off her glasses, perhaps because they were getting steamed up, and was now blinking myopically in his direction. Captax thought he had never seen her looking so beautiful. His heart gave a great bound as he moved towards her.

As they kissed, she moved her body to and fro in his arms in a way that suggested impatience to be released, as if she had left something boiling over on the stove. But he knew it was contrived; he had discovered that the happier Janet was, the more she felt impelled to surrender completely, the more she went through these non-realistic motions of wishing only to humour him.

They had been living together in his flat for just seven days.

'Darling,' he groaned, aching with happiness.

'I've been cooking like mad,' she said, twisting. 'You'd better be hungry.'

'Hungry——' Captax choked, kissing her cannibalistically.

'And I had to spend some *more* money,' she went on, pretending to ignore his embrace. 'You just didn't have *any* equipment . . . I suppose you lived on *eggs*.'

'That's right,' said Captax, getting his mouth free momentarily. 'Eggs and bought cake.'

'Ugh!' she said, letting her simulated disgust at his diet interweave contrapuntally with her real pleasure at his kisses. Captax felt as if the ventricles of his heart were choked with dead leaves. Fearing a seizure, he released Janet who moved away slowly enough to underline the artificiality of her impatient flutterings.

Left alone in the living-room, Captax poured out two shots of whisky, mixed one with the amount of soda Janet liked, and drank off the other with a practised gulp. He had had a hard day in the laboratory, and the lunch hour had been no relaxation, for he had spent it in a frustrating interview with the lawyer who was, he hoped, going to handle Janet's divorce. Strictly speaking, as the lawyer had pointed out at three-minute intervals throughout their discussion, Captax was not supposed to be doing anything in the matter. 'You ought to be waiting for the other party to proceed,' the man had said, so many times that Captax had begun to feel that he would never again lie down to sleep without hearing that phrase, *waiting for the other party to proceed*, grinding on and on in his head. But in the end the lawyer, who was a personal acquaintance, had agreed to get things moving as soon as George Links communicated with him and put the case in his hands. Puzzle: find George Links. He was not at the cottage, and a telephone call to Mr. Cropper's office had drawn only the unhelpful information that he had asked for a short holiday 'for reasons of health' and disappeared — where to, they either could not or would not say.

Captax sighed and poured himself a second whisky. Why the hell didn't George come out from wherever he was hiding and let them get going? He didn't want Janet, did he? Well then, let him get out of her light. He, Captax, wanted to marry Janet as soon as possible. As long as they were merely living together, he could not quite relax. He was so much in love with Janet that he could scarcely bring himself to believe that she loved him too. Any morning he might wake up and find that it was all a dream. Especially during the long days in the laboratory, he urgently needed something — a marriage certificate, for instance — that he could take out of his pocket now and again, to reassure him by its prosaic reality that Janet actually did exist and had entered his life with the intention of staying in it.

Meanwhile, a desert of time stretched ahead, even after it had pleased George to show himself and begin operations. God, how snarled up it all was!

Janet reappeared, carrying dishes; as he watched her

setting out their meal, Captax felt his veins fill with pure happiness. Already a husband, he noted serenely her every movement, the order in which she brought out the various dishes (those most quickly-cooling came last), and the slight frown which proclaimed her unself-conscious absorption in what she was doing.

'Come along,' she said, impersonally; clearly her whole attention was on the food. Captax approached.

'What is it?' he asked respectfully, eyeing the central dish.

'Veal à la Bretonne: I hope you like it.'

'I don't think I've ever had it,' he said humbly.

Their eyes met and they burst out laughing. It was a scene they had repeated, quite spontaneously, every evening that week. Each day, Janet had gone out shopping; each evening, Captax had returned to a meal unfamiliar to him. The rest of the conversational set-piece was, by now, automatic.

'What a marvellous cook you are.'

'I'm quite an ordinary cook. I never do anything really unusual. It's just that you've always lived so wretchedly, my poor sweet.'

Captax, this evening, started on his meal without going through the rest of the routine. But the antiphon echoed, nevertheless, in his mind. He *had* lived wretchedly. His obsessively demanding research work had claimed most of his energy, and the rest had been frittered away on his untidy, purposeless emotional life: not so much being expended as simply leaking away through the interstices in his loosely-woven existence. Now, however, he ate his Veal à la Bretonne with a new air of settled resolution. He would be no longer a mere research-machine, content to fill up his leisure hours with frippets like Barbara Bone and second-raters like George Links. He would be Fredric Captax, sleek, cared-for, a weighty citizen, respected by all, married to the sweetest wife you could picture.

As he ate he glanced round the flat. It had never looked so pleasant and habitable. His suit no longer hung on the wall, nor his dressing-gown on the back of the door. He had always found the storage-space insufficient, but it had taken Janet no time at all to conjure everything into its most fitting place, and now there seemed to be room and to spare, not only for his possessions but for the feminine accoutrements she had gone out and bought for herself.

What a wonderful thing a woman was!

Janet, helping herself to some veal, caught the look in his eyes and smiled.

'What are you thinking?'

'Guess what,' he murmured.

Bang! At the flat door. Captax jumped.

'Blast whoever this is,' he said, getting up. 'Probably some blasted tradesman delivering a——'

He wrenched open the front door. Confronting him were two people: Mrs. Edwards, his charwoman, and a man he did not know.

Captax's first thought was that he must have forgotten to leave Mrs. Edwards her money, and that she had called on her way somewhere else to pick it up. He opened his mouth to say, 'Did I forget your money this week?' but had hardly begun on the 'Did' when Mrs. Edwards said grimly:

'Oh, so you're in, Mr. Captax. My 'usband and I wanted a bit of a talk with you, if you can spare us a minute of your time.'

'By all means,' muttered Captax, nonplussed. Mrs. Edwards, a small, pinched-looking woman in a grey raincoat, was staring at him with her lips compressed to vanishing-point. Her husband, as far as he could be seen in the dim light, was a big, featureless oaf. He wore a cap and muffler and looked utterly anonymous.

'We'll step inside, if you *don't* mind,' said Mrs. Edwards aggressively.

Captax stood aside to let them pass. Her manner was beginning to annoy him; he could feel his happiness and good temper draining away. 'Let me take your hat and coat,' he said satirically. But the irony of being treated like an invited guest was lost on Mrs. Edwards. 'Along 'ere, Bert,' she said to her husband, who obediently shambled after her towards the living-room door.

Damn it! Captax thought. It was true that his flat contained only the one room in which it was possible to receive visitors — the rest being kitchen, bathroom and bedroom — but all the same he thought it unwarrantably cool of Mrs. Edwards to go sailing in. When he had first allowed the pair of them over his doorstep, it had been with some vague idea of having a short, business-like consultation in the entrance hall. Angrily, he brushed past Mrs. Edwards as she was going through the door, and preceded her into the room.

'Do carry on eating, Janet,' he said. 'I'll be with you in a minute — I expect Mrs. Edwards just wants to settle some quite small point——'

'Oh, you expect that, do you?' Mrs. Edwards said, intensifying her grimness. Captax motioned her to a chair, but she ignored him. Taking up an aggressive stance, hands on hips, in the centre of the room, she began staring fixedly at Janet.

'Well, now we can at least say we've got it all out in the open,' she said. 'At least she's 'ere for me to 'ave a good look at her.'

'What the devil do you mean?' demanded Captax.

'That's right, use strong language,' said Mrs. Edwards, nodding as if he had confirmed a prediction of hers. 'One thing leads to another, I dare say.'

Janet had laid down her knife and was leaning back in her chair as if needing support. Captax saw with pain the steam rising from the food she had so lovingly prepared.

'Look here, Mrs. Edwards, we're in the middle of a meal,' he said abruptly. 'If you've got anything to ask me or tell me, please get on with it — it's a most inconvenient time to——'

'Inconvenient!' Mrs. Edwards interrupted with a short, scornful laugh. 'Yes, I dare say it's inconvenient. I don't suppose you care much for visitors just now.'

'Get on with it, can't you?' Captax cried in desperation.

Without answering, Mrs. Edwards folded her arms across her prim little bosom and stood looking first at Janet and then at Captax. Her husband, standing two paces behind her and one pace to the side, seemed like the statue of a man made out of some unsuitable material such as cork.

'I'll get on with it,' said Mrs. Edwards at last. 'I shan't need to keep you long from whatever it is you're doing.'

'You can see perfectly well that what we're doing is to eat some food, which is going cold all the time you're keeping me standing here,' said Captax bitterly. 'Janet, do go on,' he pleaded, turning to her. 'I'll try and get Mrs. Edwards to say what she has to say and leave us in peace.'

'Peace — that's a good one,' Mrs. Edwards shrilled, beginning to break out of her false calm. 'It's not for the sinners of this world to talk about peace!'

The change of tone was so abrupt that it startled Captax. He stared at the woman, entirely unprepared for what she might do next.

'I come here as a decent clean-living woman,' said Mrs. Edwards loudly, fixing her eyes on Captax. 'I work 'ere and keep this place decent for you and it's 'eaven knows what a pigsty it'd be without me.'

'All right, all right,' Captax tried to break in.

'But the line 'as to be drawn somewhere. I'm a married woman with a duty towards my husband.'

At this reference to Mr. Edwards, Captax could not resist glancing in his direction, to see if the momentary play of the spotlight would stimulate him into any sign of life. But he merely stood in his appointed place, large, immobile, inert. An oaf, thought Captax, but not a likeable oaf.

'My 'usband allows me to come out to work,' Mrs. Edwards continued, 'to turn an honest penny. I'm not ashamed of being a working woman.'

'Oh, *get on!*' Captax shouted. 'Who said anything about being ashamed?'

'Nobody — yet,' said Mrs. Edwards, seizing her advantage with the traditional quick wit of the Cockney. 'But they should 'ave. Bein' ashamed is just exactly what I'm 'ere to talk about.'

By now, Captax could see what was coming, but he

parried bravely with, 'Why, what are you ashamed of?'

'Nothing,' said Mrs. Edwards promptly. 'It's you that's ashamed. Or if you're not, it's the worse for you.

'I come 'ere in the usual way, Tuesday morning, to do my work,' she continued after a short, dramatic pause, 'and what do I find? Nobody in, o' course, but plenty of *signs*.'

She brought out the word *signs* as if it were some obscenity which she could hardly force herself to utter. Actually, as Captax realized, she was referring simply to the few neatly folded clothes, the few feminine jars and boxes tidily arrayed in the bathroom, which were all Janet had imported.

'Oh, it's no good trying to pull the wool over *my* eyes,' said Mrs. Edwards, openly addressing Janet. 'I could see at once 'e'd got a woman living 'ere.'

Janet spoke, so quietly that Captax could only just make out her words.

'I wasn't hiding away.'

'The worse for you,' Mrs. Edwards repeated, her voice climbing unsteadily. 'You ought to 'ave been ashamed to leave your signs for a decent married woman to see.'

'Look here, I've had enough of this,' said Captax, his face crimson. He could hardly hear his own voice for the blood pounding in his ears. 'That'll do, Mrs. Edwards. I understand that you'll no longer be working for me. If I owe you any money, I'll——'

'I wouldn't take it, if you did!' cried Mrs. Edwards passionately. 'My husband wouldn't allow me to! That's why I brought 'im round with me, to make it clear that as a decent married woman I 'ave to think of my 'usband — and he just wouldn't allow me to go on workin' 'ere — *cleanin' up after a tart,*' she finished venomously.

With the word *tart,* the scene dissolved. It was as if no one could think of anything further to say or do. Captax walked mechanically to the front door and opened it; as he walked, his brain dully turned over and over, forming the resolution to attack the woman physically if she did not leave at once, and rely on doing as much damage as possible before her husband had time to intervene. In the event, however, husband and wife simply walked out without a word or gesture. Mr. Edwards had, in fact, shown a flicker of expression a moment before, when his wife had declared herself unable to accept Captax's money. A faint shadow of bewilderment had stolen across his brow, and it was still there as he obediently followed the small, jerking figure of his wife across the threshold and out.

Captax slowly went back into the living-room. Janet was sitting absolutely still in her chair, with the ruins of their dinner, still faintly steaming, in front of her. He moved towards her, but she held up one hand and said, 'No, please.'

'No what?'

'Just for a minute — don't come near me.'

Captax sank down on the sofa. He wondered what to do. If only Janet would cry, the way ahead would be clear. On the other hand, it was impossible to laugh the situation off, to assume a cheerfulness that neither of them could possibly feel.

'I feel as if I'd failed you,' he said miserably. She did not answer. *Why 'as if'?* he asked himself. *You have failed her. You've stood by and let her be insulted.*

A long time passed, or seemed to. At last he heard Janet moving. He looked up. She was clearing away the remnants of the food, stacking the cold dishes, tidying the table.

An instinct warned him to keep still. Janet was recovering balance in her own way. If she did not need him, that was a pity, but there it was. He rolled over on to his back and closed his eyes.

He heard Janet washing the dishes and putting them away. It took a long time. He thought of all the time it had taken her to cook the meal, and now she was clearing away its wreckage, hardly tasted. Mrs. Edwards loomed in his imagination as a figure of monstrous destructiveness. Groaning inwardly, Captax cursed the woman, cursed himself for having allowed her an unrestricted platform. *The sinners of this world!* he thought. *May she find out, one day, what trouble really is!*

The springs of the sofa shifted a little. Cautiously, Captax opened his eyes. Janet was sitting by his side, looking at him.

'Well?' he managed to say.

'What do *you* feel like?' she asked.

He considered a moment.

'Like a patch of grass that's had the lawn-roller standing on it.'

'But the roller's been moved away now — hasn't it?' she asked quickly.

He nodded. 'And you?'

'The same. I felt so utterly *bruised*, after that dreadful woman had — but slowly it's beginning to heal.'

They were silent for a few minutes, then:

'Fredric.'

'Yes, sweetheart?'

'You remember — what she called me?'

'Don't think about it,' he said hotly.

'No, but . . .'

'But *what?*'

'Do *you* think I'm one?'

'Good God, no,' he said, shocked, sitting up straight.

'Are you sure?' she asked softly, her face hidden.

'*Sure?* I love you, don't you understand?'

After a moment she answered:

'Yes . . . but you could love me and still think . . .'

'Think what?'

'That I was a tart,' she said flatly.

Captax reached out to take her in his arms.

'No, please,' she said. 'Not yet.'

'I only want to be near you.'

She lay quiescent, neither encouraging nor rebuffing him. Patient, he had the sense not to touch her.

A pause again, then:

'Fredric.'

'Darling?'

'Do you really love me?'

'What would you like me to do,' he asked passionately, 'to prove it?'

'And would you still love me,' she persisted, 'if I were what that woman called me?'

'It's an absurd question. You couldn't be.'

'Would you?'

'It's absurd. I can't take the question seriously enough to answer it.'

'Why is it absurd? I left my husband and came to you. That's what they call adultery.'

'Words, words,' Captax cried impatiently. 'Put it

173

another way, use other terms, and it takes on a different colour altogether.'

'Well, go on. Use the other terms you can so easily find.'

'With pleasure. You were married to a man who didn't know his own good luck. You loved him and gave him everything, and he hadn't the sense to value it. After years of giving and not being appreciated, you found out, quite by chance, that he was making love to another woman.'

Without moving a muscle she asked, in a tiny voice, 'And what happened then?'

'What happened then was that your heart dried up. It contracted to the size of a prune. But fortunately you didn't have to continue long in that state.'

'No?'

'No. Because there was already another man who loved you. You went to him and he told you of his love.'

'And what happened then?'

'Your heart expanded again. It drank in the love he offered you, and at once it went back to its normal size and shape.'

'And what was it like then?' she asked, like a child being told a story.

'What was it like?' he repeated meditatively. 'It was like a pium, compared with a prune.'

'Or a grape compared with a raisin?'

'Just so,' he said, taking her hands.

She looked up at him, and he saw confidence stealing back into her face.

'Darling Fredric,' she said softly. Then the doorbell rang.

174

'Holy Christ!' said Captax, disengaging himself. 'Whoever *this* is is going to get the treatment.'

He stumped out. Janet, listening, heard the door open and a feminine voice, not known to her, say, 'Can I come in?'

'Oh, for Christ's sake, *no*,' she heard Captax groan.

'Yes, *please*,' said Barbara Bone. 'I got your letter, and I don't want to go on with it any more than you do, but I wanted to ask you——'

'I've nothing to tell you!' Captax interrupted loudly. 'For God's sake go away and leave me in peace!'

'I wanted to ask you about George!' Mrs. Bone yelped, raising her voice to correspond with his. As Captax had fallen silent, the words rang through the flat with unforgettable loudness.

Janet rose from the sofa. 'All right, Fredric,' she called. 'Let's have it. Bring her in: let me see who it is who wants to ask you about George.'

Barbara Bone, stiffening to attention, looked up at Captax enquiringly. But he could say nothing. The situation had, at last, overwhelmed his inventiveness — overwhelmed, even, his willingness to be inventive. His hands fell limply to his sides.

'Who is it?' Barbara Bone asked.

Captax, his face a collapsed mask of helplessness, jerked his head in the direction of the living-room.

'Bring her *in*,' Janet called, insistently.

Barbara Bone hesitated for an instant, then shrugged, as if to indicate that there was no point in going back now and she might as well run headlong into whatever new complication awaited her. With quick, precise little steps, she walked past Captax and into the living-room.

Janet was sitting at the table, her chin resting on her clasped hands. She looked up at Barbara Bone like a prospective employer at the beginning of an interview.

'Come in,' she said, 'and sit down if you're tired. I think we might as well all three settle down and have a nice clearing-up talk.'

Barbara Bone seemed determined to prove Janet's equal in self-confidence. The only difference was that in her case the poise was slightly jaunty and with a streak of defiance in it, whereas Janet's was simply the worn-down bleakness of one who can no longer find the energy for embarrassment or evasion.

Captax, following Barbara in, was struck by this contrast as he looked from one to the other. Digging backward into himself, he tried to find the materials for a similar display on his own part. But it seemed that the women had absorbed every available scrap of self-confidence in the atmosphere, leaving him with nothing he could extract.

Barbara Bone sat down on the sofa. She managed to make sitting down look a less comfortable position than standing up, but at least it was a move in the game.

'Go ahead,' she said carelessly. 'I don't mind how much clearing up goes on. I came to ask Fredric a question and I'm prepared to ask him in front of anybody. All the same, it would be nice to know something about what's going on.'

'Like what?' said Captax, his voice sounding hollow and unreal by contrast with the bird-tones of the women.

'Like who this is, for instance,' said Mrs. Bone, nodding towards Janet.

'She's——' Captax began, but a fatal indecision — not knowing whether to introduce Janet as his future wife,

or George Links's erstwhile wife, or simply by name —
robbed him of his advantage, and Janet took over.

'It's a name you'll know,' she said coolly. 'Links.'

Barbara Bone remained silent and motionless for a
few seconds, as if she had not heard. Then she got up,
walked to the other side of the room, and stood with her
back to the others.

'Janet's——' began Captax, trying again.

Barbara Bone swung round and stared at Janet.

'Do you live here,' she asked, 'or are you just
visiting?'

'I live here.'

'So it's true. You've left George.'

Janet shrugged minimally; the movement was just
perceptible. 'Is it important for you to know?'

'Look here——' Captax began abruptly. Both women
turned their eyes expectantly on him, but he seemed
to have nothing more to say. Struggling through to
the end of a sentence, he got as far as, 'there's a lot of
detail lying about which, if we go into it, we shall find
is obsolete.' His voice seemed to be running down like
a clockwork toy; it became slower and slower, till on
the word 'obsolete' it dragged slowly to a halt.

'All right,' said Barbara Bone, crisply taking up the
running, 'I'll go on. I seem to be the only person here
who might seem to have anything to hide. I see the
situation here; you two are living together, and George
is abandoned in a ditch somewhere.'

'We're going to get married,' Captax put in quickly.

'All right. That still leaves George stuck in a
ditch.'

Janet lifted her chin from her hands for long enough
to speak.

'Perhaps he's in the same ditch as your husband.'

'Wrong,' said Barbara Bone in the same crisp voice. 'They're both in a ditch, but it's not the same one. You're quite right to guess that I'm not particularly concerned with Evan's welfare at the moment, any more than you are with George's. But where your husband landed himself in the ditch through neglecting you, mine got there through being too damned attentive.'

'I think you're a fool, but still,' said Janet, 'I think you'll learn one day that to be too attentive is the only forgiveable fault a man can have.' Her voice, calm but weary, seemed to come from centuries of disillusion.

'You don't understand. The attentiveness wasn't in the right direction. He was more attentive to any other man I happened to have a drink with than he was to me.'

'It's the same thing. It's for your sake.'

'It's *not* the same thing. Anyway, let's get off that. We're putting our cards on the table, so let me go on and say that I've just about had enough of Evan's hysteria and his jealousies.'

'You're leaving him?'

'I haven't made up my mind yet. The main thing is to bring him to his senses first by giving him something to be jealous about. Then perhaps he'll be able to tell the difference between real worries and imaginary ones.'

Janet looked up with a small, frosty smile. 'You can't do it, can you?' she asked.

'Can't do what?'

'Can't play this game of confessions. I'm not blaming you. I don't suppose many women can. It's not really our nature. I just find it a bit amusing, that's all.'

'Amusing?' cried Barbara Bone indignantly.

'You can't have any motive for lying to anyone here. We're all three about as far astray as we can be. There can't be any comparison between us — nobody's going to say *I'm better than you are* or *You shouldn't have done that*. And you know that and yet you still can't give it to us straight.'

She paused, but Mrs. Bone said nothing.

'All this stuff about giving your husband a shock to do him good. Make him able to distinguish between this and that . . . God, how can you talk such rubbish? That isn't the way women talk to themselves — and I doubt if you could even get Fredric to think it was, never mind me.'

Barbara Bone's confidence had slipped. She was like a woman trying to hide her face in an ill-fitting mask.

'What you really mean, you poor little innocent,' Janet went on, 'is that you're tired of the man you married, or perhaps never really wanted him in the first place would be more like it, and you want to go to bed with some other men for a change, only you haven't the guts to walk out on your husband and definitely attach yourself to someone else. Or perhaps you just know there isn't any man who'd like you to attach yourself to him, however willing they all might be to sleep with you. So you dither about, making up silly little reasons and expecting us to believe them——'

'All right!' Barbara Bone cried suddenly. Her voice was full of pain, and she blinked away tears. Captax felt a surge of pity for her; this, the distressed pretty schoolgirl, was a much more genuine rôle for her, near enough to her real character to enable her to be really appealing. Janet, with her executive-desk manner, her folded hands and her coldly fantastic spectacle-frames, was the cool one. But she was the one he loved — *wasn't she?* His brain seemed full of mad bees.

Barbara Bone, evidently under intolerable tension, jumped to her feet, paced quickly up and down the room for a few seconds, then turned abruptly to face Janet.

'So that's what you find me,' she said, speaking so rapidly that her words slurred into one another. 'A poor little innocent. Whereas you're the one who's been everywhere and done everything.'

'I didn't say that.'

'No, but you meant it. My God, what sort of a position d'you think it puts you in, now you've left George and come to live with Fredric? D'you think it gives you the right to look down on everyone from a tremendous height?'

'We're going to be married,' said Captax again. The words had come to seem to him a kind of rune which, spoken enough times, might somehow make sense of the nightmare.

'Don't you butt in, Fredric,' said Mrs. Bone contemptuously. 'You're just afraid I'll tell her about you and me, that's all.'

'You don't have to,' said Janet, looking icily straight in front of her. 'From the way he's been fidgeting ever since you came in, I could see there was something he was afraid you'd spill. And it didn't take much imagination to think what it might be.'

'All right,' said Captax, irritated into frankness. 'The way you both discuss me as if I were a piece of furniture, you make me feel there's no point in being tactful any more——'

'*Tactful!*' Janet cried. Throwing back her head, she laughed with what seemed genuine bitter amusement. 'That's the funniest thing I've ever heard. Tactful! Congratulations, Fredric! To be able to think about tact at a time like this really must take some doing.'

'So I did have an affair with Barbara,' Captax persisted, scowling. 'A brief, abortive one that never had time to amount to anything——'

'Time?' said Barbara Bone, stopping short in her pacing. 'Don't let's bring time into it. It wouldn't have amounted to anything in a million years.'

'——and was broken off by me, in writing, as soon as you came into my life,' Captax went on, ignoring the interruption, his eyes fixed on Janet.

'Yes, a pompous little note,' Barbara Bone said viciously, 'that I found waiting for me one morning at the office where I work. I've got it here, if you'd like to see it,' she said to Janet. Opening her handbag, she took out a letter and held it up. Captax started forward angrily.

'So you work in an office, do you?' said Janet meditatively. 'It certainly helps to explain the grudge against your husband, if he couldn't even support you.'

Mrs. Bone sank down in a chair. 'My God,' she said, in the tone of someone being shown a photograph of some hideous act of cruelty. 'My God. There isn't anything you won't stoop to, is there?' Her manner was impersonal, as if contemplating sympathetically an outrage done to someone she did not know. 'Why do you hate me so much? It isn't because of Fredric, obviously.'

'And why is that *obvious*?'

'For one thing, I don't believe you're in love with him. For another, even if you were it wouldn't make you hate me as much as that, just because I was mixed up with him before you were.'

'You're wrong,' said Janet, coolly, as if it hardly concerned her. 'I don't hate you. I've no reason to have any reaction to you one way or another. All that interests me is that you've come round here to get something — I don't know what — and if one could only get you to be honest, and get on with it, we might be done with the whole business more quickly.'

Mrs. Bone stood perfectly still, in the middle of the room, as if all movement had now become superfluous. When she spoke, it was on a dead monotone.

'Yes, we'll be done with the business,' she said. 'I came round to know if Fredric could help me to find George. I'd heard from my fool of a husband, who came running to me with the news as if it were something I'd jump for joy about, that you'd abandoned him.'

'And you thought the office of sweet consoler might be vacant?'

'I hate you,' Barbara Bone said calmly, looking at Janet appraisingly, as if trying to guess her weight. 'I hate you so much that I'm glad you've finished with George.'

'I suppose you'll tell me you love George?'

'I shan't tell *you* anything. I've nothing to tell either of you. I just want to know if you've any idea where George is, and whether, if so, it's any use asking you to tell me. You might as well; if you've finished with him, you can hardly care who gets him.'

Captax wanted to interrupt, to say or do something that would break into this iron fugue. But he could think of no rune strong enough to be heard in that grey, icy air. He stood, helpless, feeling himself consigned to the background.

Janet rose, and walked across the room to get her handbag. Clicking it open, she took out a card, which she offered to Barbara Bone between the first two fingers of her extended hand.

'What's this?' said Mrs. Bone, looking down at it without moving.

'Take it and see.'

She took it. 'Cropper, Fulbelow and Jackson.'

'George's firm. One of their business cards. You can trace him from there, if you persist.'

Janet brought out the word *persist* so that it was like a slap across the face. Captax felt himself wincing. His limbs started into movement.

'For Christ's sake,' he cried, lurching forward. 'Janet, what are you doing?'

'Doing?' she said, turning to him with her perfect-secretary look, the one he hated so much. 'I'm simply doing what's asked of me. I'm helping your ex-mistress to get in touch with my husband.'

'Is that really what's asked of you?' he said dully.

'Well, settle it your own way, the two of you,' said Mrs. Bone. She suddenly seemed brighter and more confident. 'I'm glad I came, even though it's all so horrible and I'm so relieved to be going again. You see, I really genuinely want to find out where George is and see what I can do for him.'

'Oh, as to that,' said Janet in her precise, cold voice, 'there's no mystery; it's clear enough what you can *do* for him.'

Barbara Bone walked over to the door as if she had not heard. In the doorway, she turned.

'You heard that, Fredric?' she said, facing him and jerking her head towards Janet. 'You understand the kind of woman you've got yourself tied up with?'

She disappeared through the doorway, her footsteps clicked across the hall, the front door opened and shut. She was gone.

Captax and Janet, avoiding each other's eyes, stood together in a room full of loneliness. Minutes seemed to tick by. Captax struggled for something to say, but there seemed to be no thought, no words, anywhere in the universe — not a wisp of rope he could throw across the emptiness between them.

At last Janet said, 'I think I'd like a bath.'

'I'll run the water,' said Captax at once. He hurried briskly, thankfully, out of the room.

⋆ XII ⋆

IMMEDIATELY on entering the saloon bar, George
Links saw Captax, his face lumpy and pallid under
the uneasy light bulbs, sitting in his usual corner.
A glass of red wine stood untouched before him; his
eyes were fixed on a letter which he incessantly took
from, and put back into, its envelope.

Captax showed, at first, no consciousness of who it
was who approached and sat down opposite him. He
ceased, however, to take out and replace the letter.
Letting it lie on the table beside his glass, he kept his
eyes on it for a moment, then raised them to meet
those of George Links, and said, 'Well?'

'Where is she?' George Links asked.

Captax dropped his eyes to the letter again. 'You
guess.'

'At home, I suppose, cooking your supper.'

Before answering, Captax drank from his glass.
'Warm,' he said. 'This time twenty-four hours ago
you'd have been right. She did cook my supper
yesterday. Mackerel *aux fines herbes*, it was. Very
nice: I'd never had it before. She was a good cook,
wasn't she?'

'Was?' George Links asked.

'Yes. She gave me things most times I hadn't had
before. We had Veal à la Bretonne one night,' said

Captax, remembering. 'But I didn't get a chance to eat much of it. Some people came.'

'Well,' said George Links patiently, 'and where is she to-night?'

Captax nodded towards the letter lying on the table. 'Gone,' he said.

'Gone?'

Captax picked up his glass and drank again.

'For good?' George Links persisted dully.

'For good or evil.'

They sat silent for a moment, then George Links said, 'That wraps it up.'

'For me, yes,' said Captax. 'But I don't see how it affects you.'

'No, you wouldn't.'

There was another silence.

'Well, go on, talk,' said Captax. 'Go and get yourself a drink and start talking. The evening stretches before us, and I can't see that either of us has anything better to do.'

George Links leaned forward with a flicker of urgency that spent itself as quickly as it came. 'Don't you know where she is?' he asked.

'No: why, do you?'

'Of course not.'

'Well, then,' said Captax impatiently, 'go and get yourself a drink and come back and talk instead of asking dam' fool questions.'

George Links still did not move. 'Why did she set that Bone girl on to me?' he said suddenly.

'Oh, so she found you, did she? That was about a week ago. Did it take her long?'

'She told me Janet had given her the first clue,'

said George Links, ignoring the question. 'Why did
she do that?'

Captax considered. 'I suppose the motive was to
give the girl as much help as possible in bitching up her
own marriage.'

'Why — did she hate her?'

'Not her,' said Captax, shaking his head. 'It was
the husband she hated.'

'The husband? Evan? Why should she . . .'

'Didn't you know,' said Captax, staring at him,
'that it was this Evan that first tipped her off about you
and Ruth?'

'Good Christ,' said George Links. He paused for a
moment, thinking. 'I suppose that explains a lot. It
certainly makes me see why she should have sicked this
girl on to me. So she hates him, does she? But why —
unless she loves me?'

'She *did* love you, that I do know,' said Captax. 'My
impression was that the shock killed that. But of course
the hatred of the man who'd blabbed might survive
where the love didn't. It might take over, so to speak,
from the love.'

'Did she love you?' George Links asked, impersonally.

'I don't suppose so.'

'Why did she come to live with you, then?'

'Why, why, why,' said Captax drearily. 'Why did
she come to me, why did she leave me, why did she
stay a fortnight instead of one day or ten years? I can
only make guesses. Probably she needed a man to
comfort her, which God knows I was ready to do, and
probably she chose me for reasons that were partly
vengeful.' He spoke as if mechanically developing a

thesis that did not in any way concern him. 'I daresay
she wanted to destroy me — unconsciously, or at least
partly so — for the part I'd played in helping you to
hoodwink her.'

'To hoodwink her,' said George Links. 'My God,
it seems almost impossible, now, to think back on all
that. The phoney visits to that chap — what was his
name? Volumis. Getting you to impersonate him.
It just doesn't seem to belong in the same lifetime.'

'It doesn't,' said Captax heavily. 'We've changed
lifetimes. People can, I realize that now. After all,
old Cowley did, didn't he?'

'So you know about that too, do you?'

'Yes. I went round to see him after Janet trans-
ferred to me. I didn't want to *consult* him, necessarily,
but I felt the need of someone solid to talk to.'

'And you also thought you'd go and see for yourself
whether I'd managed to get Ruth away from him.'

'*Touché*,' said Captax. 'The fact is, I wanted the
whole thing cleared up, and I knew that was the place
to apply.'

They sat immersed in their own thoughts for some
time. The conversation seemed to be over, but each
knew that in fact it had not yet begun. The preliminaries had been cleared away, contact had been
established, and the deep torrential flow, which both
so painfully desired, was almost tapped.

'Where are you living?' Captax asked.

'For the moment, in one of those fly-blown little
hotels near the B.M.'

'Well, come home with me,' said Captax, rising.
'We can boil an egg or something. It'll be better than
sitting about here.'

George Links nodded and stood up. 'All right,' he said. .   .   .   .

Midwinter stillness gripped the quiet street in the neighbourhood of Swiss Cottage. As Janet walked deliberately along the pavement, looking for the right number, she was aware of the merciless clarity of the frosty air. Let it be so! Clarity was what she welcomed — and if it had to be merciless, who cared? Within her bones she felt an ice-hard marrow that matched the cold sky and the hard earth.

It must be somewhere here, where these Cowleys lived. She had got the address from the telephone book. Somehow that cool, precise little entry — *Cowley, E. J.*, *such-and-such an address, NW 3* — was the first thing that had brought a touch of everyday reality to the situation. Till then, it had all seemed unreal, a dream, a set of fantastic alternatives that need not be seriously acted on. But at last she had taken up the bulky volume A - D, and found the name; and from that moment on, her nightmare was waiting to be enacted in the ordinary daylight.

To confront the Cowleys — that was as far as her plan extended. Plan? She admitted to herself, as she walked along, that it was less a plan than a compulsion. Since the fatal interview with Evan Bone, when she had clutched her Christmas parcels in hands that seemed made of brittle ice, her life had been a series of compulsions. To visit Captax, to stay on within his protection, to leave him, all had been compulsive actions: she had simply been impelled by the unmoored thrashing instincts within her. And now, the strongest compulsion of all, the one she had most determinedly struggled against: to enter the Cowley household, to see the woman who had bewitched George and taken him away from her, who had made him capable of such appalling, destructive doubleness. Or, failing that, to confront the husband — to see what kind of a man it was who, entrusted with the custody of a dangerous animal, permitted it to walk free and cause havoc in the lives of innocent people: while he, blind fool, gave his energies to offering advice to these same people on their metaphysical problems. Confront him? It might be possible, Janet thought with a cold uprush of malicious pleasure, to go some distance towards unsettling him — entangling him, even. That would be perfect: to leave the woman lonely and bewildered, puzzling in an empty bed, or beside the thoughtless sleeping carcase of her man, asking herself what had happened to take away the warmth that should have been hers. Why not, after all? He was no doubt a secluded, bookish fellow, well inoculated against life; probably no woman had ever made a direct advance to him in his life — a direct incitement to promiscuity. Let it happen. If he were in by himself, there would be no harm in beginning straight away to see what destruction she could cause.

Here was the right number. This must be the house, the scene of her own defeat — that defeat which had taken place silently, unknown to her, while she waited at home in love and confidence. Now she felt justified; her timidity fell away; the remedy — or rather the revenge, since it was past remedy — was to make this same house the scene of a whole campaign in which the battle she had lost would be seen merely as the first.

Up the garden path she walked, between the iron-hard flower-beds from which winter had stripped away all caprice and profusion. With an unwavering, unfeeling hand, she rang the bell.

·   ·   ·   ·   ·

'Anyway, round comes this girl to my hotel,' said George Links, pushing away the plate from which he had been eating bread and cheese. 'She's tracked me down — it wasn't too difficult, as the office got sick of answering enquiries and just gave in and told her where I was. So in she comes, one afternoon, when I was just lying on the bed.'

'Asleep?' Captax asked, pouring out beer.

'No, just lying there . . . I seemed to spend all day, after about noon, just lying on my back, trying to collect my impressions. I couldn't, though. It was like gathering up a lot of odds and ends and putting them in a sack — only the sack had no bottom, and every time there they were again, dispersed and lying about everywhere.'

'Go on about the girl.'

'Oh, yes, the girl,' said George Links flatly, as if remembering the details of some boring piece of technical procedure. 'Well, she didn't waste any time on formalities or talking about the weather. She was in a terrific state of excitement. She'd found me at last, and she was going to show me that there was someone who cared for me — all that sort of thing.'

'Rather touching, surely?' said Captax, eyeing George Links curiously.

'Touching?' George Links asked, as if uncertain of the meaning of the word. 'Oh, God, yes; I suppose so. Anyway, she was fairly steamed up. I think if I'd given her any encouragement she'd have attached herself to me there and then. Walked out on her husband and taken over lock, stock and barrel.'

'Except, of course,' said Captax severely, 'that she wouldn't have thought of it as attaching herself to you. She thought of you as down and beaten, and she wanted to help you up.'

'Well, put it any way you like.'

'I'm simply helping you to see it from the girl's point of view. The way you put it, you make her sound simply like a parasite.'

'Oh, all right, only let me get on with the story: you asked me for it, after all. Well, naturally I wasn't having that.'

Captax looked as if he would have liked to interrupt again, but controlled himself and was silent.

'Well, as we stood, I just couldn't think what to do. My heart didn't exactly leap up when I saw this girl, but on the other hand I did have a kind of feeling that any offer of help, coming at a time when I'd been more or less giving up hope, seemed — what shall I say . . . *meant*. I had an almost superstitious feeling that I oughtn't to turn it down.'

'Superstitious, eh?' said Captax, nodding and compressing his lips.

'Well, without too much searching for the exact word, I felt a strong impulse to accept what this girl was offering to me, and yet I didn't know *how*, quite. I mean the practicalities of the thing were obscure. What did I propose to *do* with her? What did she want us to do? Elope? And get me sued by her husband as well as everything else? And what did she expect me to do about supporting her?'

'She wasn't thinking any of those things,' said Captax. 'She just wanted to help you.'

'All right, don't keep putting in that kind of comment. I know. Anyway, this is what went on in my mind. I just couldn't move, in any direction. So I told her to come back the next day and I'd see what seemed best to do.'

Captax got up from his chair and walked across to the other side of the room, as if trying to get as far away from George Links as possible. Then he came back, stood looking down at George Links for a moment, and sat down again.

'You sent her back to her husband?' he said at last.

'Yes, yes, yes, for Christ's sake,' said George Links irritably. 'Don't keep interrupting me. I sent her back to her husband, if you like. Actually I just told her to come back the next day. God damn it, she could have gone and spent the night with her old Mum for all I knew.'

'Or cared.'

'Or cared. And let that be your last interruption, if you want to hear the rest of what happened. Right. So I sent her away for twenty-four hours. And when she came back the next afternoon, I still hadn't got it settled in my mind. It wasn't just that I couldn't think what to do with her; I couldn't think what to do, full stop. The larger framework was obscure, so naturally the place of each individual detail was obscure too.'

'Each individual detail,' said Captax, half under his breath, nodding again.

'But there was one thing I was quite clear about. She could give me very valuable help in one respect at least. You see, I wanted to go . . . down to the cottage. I didn't ever want to stay there any length of time, but I had to go back for a few hours anyway, if only to pack a case with a few necessities, documents and one thing and another, and make arrangements for the charwoman to come in and keep the place clean while it was being sold, and that kind of thing. I'd been trying to face the prospect for some days, but every time I thought about it my mind just went blank. It was one of those things that are just too much to face.' George Links looked straight ahead of him, woodenly, as he spoke. His voice sounded as if he were repeating sentences in a language that had no meaning for him. 'Then of course it struck me. If I went down there with this Bone girl, she'd be a sort of emotional bodyguard. I mean, to put it another way, she'd insulate me. Help to lay Janet's ghost.'

'That's three figures of speech one after another,' said Captax coldly. 'A bodyguard, an insulation, an exorcist of ghosts. Are they alternatives? Can one choose?'

'*Similia similibus curantur,*' said George Links defiantly. 'That means "like drives out like" in Latin, Fredric. Shall I try and think of formulations in a few other languages, or will you let me get on with the story?'

'Like, eh?' said Captax, as if committing a key expression to memory. 'All right, go on, George. Tell me how like drove out like. Tell me how your bodyguard insulated the ghost.'

'We set off at once. I checked out of my hotel — I didn't feel in any mood to have trailing roots, any place where I was expected back, any arrangements I'd have to cancel or stick to. I felt I had enough roots, dead and half-dead, trailing after me as it was.'

'So you went off to Paddington Station.'

'We went off to Paddington Station. The Bone girl was all for helping me to get free of the little home. She didn't even kick at the thought of spending a night there, which I told her she'd probably have to do. Anyway, we got to the station for the three-fifteen. I was trying to make my mind as blank as possible. I kept telling myself that it was the last time I'd have to do it. It was shaking me up pretty badly, but I kept control partly by dwelling on how it was the last time, and partly by taking everything in as flat and matter-of-fact a way as I could — it was just an ordinary railway platform, just a train similar to thousands I'd seen before, and so on. And by holding on hard to that kind of support I got as far as booking the tickets and finding the right platform. I even got the girl settled in a compartment. Then I looked at my watch and saw that the train didn't go for seven minutes.'

'And what was peculiar about that?'

'Nothing, except that the whole story would have been different without that seven-minute gap. If something had just happened to slow us up — if the bus had been caught in a traffic jam, for instance, on the way to Paddington, or if there'd been a queue at the booking-office . . . as it was, I suddenly felt I couldn't stand those seven minutes. I just couldn't sit still in the train; it was beginning to drive me insane. So I told the girl I was going to buy some magazines to read in the train. It was quite true; I thought I'd take my time over choosing a few and get back just as the train was about to move.'

'Instead of which, what?'

'Instead of which, I got as far as the bookstall at the foot of Platform 1, and I was just beginning to cast an eye over the stuff they'd got, when I saw a kid. Back view. A boy of about ten.'

'Incredible,' said Captax heavily.

'He was standing with his back to me, taking the number of the shunting engine that had brought the carriages into position. And when he'd taken the number he bent down and seemed to be examining the wheels or something.'

'I've got it!' Captax exclaimed, snapping his fingers. 'You saw that kid of the Cowleys'!'

'I stood looking at his back view. It seemed to me that the back of his neck reminded me of Ruth's. It was just something about the way the head was related to the shoulders. Pure fancy, of course. But suddenly I felt as if I'd been sandbagged. It brought it all back — just the sight of that boy with an exercise book under his arm . . . of course, the kid was always hanging about stations, and I remembered him saying he hadn't got full coverage on the Western Region. Full coverage! That was the way he used to talk, you know.'

'Still does, I expect,' said Captax.

'I stood there. I couldn't move an inch. If you don't know the feeling, there's no point in trying to tell you. *I just stood there.*'

'So the train began to move,' said Captax.

'It began and it kept on. Out of the corner of my eye, I could see the carriages slowly drawing away. I managed to turn my head and look down the train. Then the Bone girl put her head out of the window. She called something — telling me to jump into one of the rear coaches, probably. I just managed a kind of shrug — I don't know what she understood by it. Nothing, I suppose. There wasn't anything I could tell her, anyway. I just meant to convey helplessness. I wanted, in a kind of way, to get on the train, but it was all so damned futile.'

'So the train pulled out with her in it?'

'Yes. And there was the shunting engine left standing by itself, and there was the kid still looking at the connecting-rods or whatever it was. And there was I still standing by the bookstall. Then the kid straightened up and turned so that I saw his face. And God almighty, Fredric, it wasn't Teddy at all. It was some other kid who didn't even look like him. This one was half a head taller and held himself quite differently. And all that guff about the back of his neck reminding me of Ruth's — it was just a hallucination.'

'In one word, you're deranged.'

'Use any word you like. To me, what became clear in that moment was that I was *finished*. That there was no point in trying to get back to normality any more. If the mere sight of a kid taking train numbers was enough to rock me like that, what was the use?'

He paused.

'Well, go on,' said Captax.

'That's all.'

Captax flushed angrily. 'No, it isn't. There's a lot more, in fact the most important part, that you haven't touched on.'

'Like what?' asked George Links indifferently.

'Like what happened to Barbara.'

George Links shrugged. 'I suppose she got off when the train stopped and got another one back.'

197

'You *suppose*, do you?' said Captax grimly. 'And what do you *suppose* she did when she got back?'

'Anything or nothing. She could have looked for me, but since I'd checked out of the hotel, and gone to another one, she naturally wouldn't find me. She might have given up and gone back to Evan.'

'Jesus Christ,' said Captax in an awe-struck voice. Glaring, he fumbled for words. But before any came to his mind the door bell rang.

'I'll have this God-damned bell disconnected, that's a promise,' said Captax, marching with hunched shoulders to the door. He did not delay, but before he reached it, even so, the bell shrilled again, to the accompaniment of loud, demented knocking.

'All right!' Captax shouted, wrenching the door open. 'What the——'

'All right, is it?' a familiar voice yelled. 'I'll bloody well all right you, you ——'

Evan Bone, his face paper-white, his eyes as pink as an albino rabbit's, projected his long body over the threshold. As he came he swung his fist wildly. More by luck than accuracy, it slammed into Captax's jaw and drove his head back into the wall.

'Mmmmmm,' said Captax through his clamped teeth. He sagged, half stunned.

George Links, startled by the yell and the double thump, hurried into the passage. Bone, who had been about to turn savagely on Captax again, swung round with an expression of ferocious triumph.

'Got you both together,' he panted. 'A gift. Shows how right I was.'

'You're drunk, aren't you?' George Links said dully. The scene ought to have roused or frightened him, but nothing seemed to matter enough. Bone was drunk, so what? He was fighting mad about that silly little heifer of his. Well, and then?

Evan Bone, lurching towards him, struck out again. As the fist came up towards him George Links saw quite clearly that it was bleeding. Then he felt it beat into the side of his face. The blow was a clumsy one; aimed presumably at the point of the jaw, it merely glanced along the jaw-line, ending up by brushing heavily past the right ear.

Mechanically, feeling that the whole scene was being enacted by puppets, and that he was watching and not even giving it his full attention, George Links drew back his fist and punched Evan Bone coldly in the midriff.

The door was open. As Bone, his mouth helplessly open, struggled to draw breath, George Links gave him a single hard push which sent him tottering out. The door-handle caught in his sleeve as he went out, and in an instant it had slammed and the flat contained two people once more. The whole scene had taken perhaps forty seconds.

Captax walked deliberately into the kitchen and turned on the cold tap. George Links heard him bathing his face. 'I've bitten my tongue,' he heard between splashes. 'God, how I hate biting my bloody tongue.'

George Links walked sadly into the living-room and sat down. He was sorry Captax had bitten his tongue, he was sorry for everybody in the world — but really, what was the difference?

* XIII *

GRIMLY, her small neat body erect and poised, Janet stared without blinking at the leaded panes of the front door. Let one of these Cowleys appear: let them show themselves, it was all she asked.

The door began to open of its own acccord, Jane fancied for a second. Then she dropped her eyes to child-level.

'Good afternoon,' said Teddy.

Janet was thrown off her stride. She had not been told of Teddy's existence. The Cowleys' son, evidently. How many others were there? Would she find the house full of children? And how would that affect the situation — would it mean readjusting her sights before firing?

Then squaring her shoulders, she dismissed the momentary hesitation. 'Is Mr. or Mrs. Cowley in?'

'My mother's out,' said Teddy with his habitual precise gravity. 'But my Dad's in. Will you come in, please?'

He stepped back politely. Janet advanced over the threshold with her mind clenched like a fist. She was on the attack, and no solemn-eyed elf was going to make her finger slacken from the trigger. She was perfectly ready, if it became necessary, to blast him together with his parents — and his brothers and sisters, too, if he had any.

'Have you any brothers and sisters?' she asked
Teddy, as he turned round from shutting the door.

The question surprised her. She felt uncollected,
rattled at the centre of that clenched mind. What could
have made her lead off with such a question?

'No, I'm the only one,' said Teddy. 'Up to now,'
he added, as if wishing to be scrupulously fair to all the
possibilities. As he spoke, he led the way across the
hall and pushed open the sitting-room door.

Janet followed, uneasily. She began to wish that she
had formed a definite plan of campaign before coming
to the house. Relying on her determination alone, she
was unprepared for the various eddies and swirls of
the situation.

And yet — she pulled herself up again — why should
she stoop to forming plans and strategies? Surely it
was enough for her to confront the woman and say,
'I'm the wife of the man you've been destructively
meddling with': or, if it was the husband, to begin
simply by asking, 'Did you know that your wife has
stolen my husband?' Then the next move could be
left to them: with the knowledge that she could handle
it, whatever it was.

Teddy was watching her. 'Would you like to sit
down?' he asked.

Without speaking, Janet chose the most upright of
the armchairs, perched rigidly on the edge of the seat,
and gazed determinedly out of the window. Teddy
must not be encouraged. She felt the danger of getting
into conversation with him; he melted her bones, and
she could not afford to have her bones melted when
there were two people she wanted to hack to pieces with
the sharp edges of them.

There was a silence, which began to creep like a fog into Janet's veins. Just as she had reached the point of deciding to end it by saying something, no matter what, Teddy, who had been watching her steadily, volunteered:

'I expect my mother'll be home quite soon.'

Unnerved, Janet turned sharply to face him.

'I thought you said your father was in already?'

'He is.'

'Well, then,' she snapped.

Teddy moved one foot slightly ahead of the other, and stood looking down at it reflectively, as if studying its effect against the pattern of the carpet.

'Is it something really important?' he asked.

Janet made a gesture of impatience and helplessness. 'I can't tell what you would think important,' she said. Odd, how one fell into this trick of talking to the child as if he were an adult! 'Please tell your father I'm here, Teddy,' she went on more softly. 'Tell him it's Mrs. Links.'

At the name, Teddy looked up from his study of shoe and carpet. 'That's two people with that name that come here,' he said. 'There's a friend of Mummy's called Mr. Links. But he doesn't live in London.'

Janet was silent.

'Mr. Links lives on the Western Region,' said Teddy, half to himself.

Janet looked out of the window again. The garden looked so dead that she could not believe it would ever be spring. The earth was like painted iron.

'I live on the Western Region, too,' she heard herself say.

'Do you live with Mr. Links?' Teddy asked, his tone expressing polite interest.

Janet stood up abruptly. 'Teddy, I'd like to go on talking to you, but I want to see your father, now, at once, please.' Her voice was jerky and sharp-edged in spite of a most determined effort to control it.

'It is something very important then,' said the boy softly.

Janet clenched and unclenched her hands. 'Yes, yes, it's something very important, only *go and fetch him.*'

Teddy still did not move. 'You see,' he explained, 'I have to ask that question because it's part of my instructions.'

'Your instructions?' she asked wearily.

'When my mother's out and there's only my Dad and me at home, I have instructions,' said Teddy. 'If my Dad isn't working, if he's knocking about the house, he answers the door. If he *is* working, I answer it, and that's what I mean about my instructions. I'm only to fetch him if it's something very important.'

'And why won't you believe me,' she said in anguish, 'that it is something important I've come about — very important?'

'I do believe you,' said Teddy politely. But she caught a watchful gleam in his round eyes. He was protecting his father, she realised. Intuitively, he had perceived that she came to bring disturbance — the kind of thing that instinct told him to direct towards his mother.

This train of thought irresistibly drew Janet away from her own hatred and determination.

'You're very proud of your father, aren't you, Teddy?' she asked.

'I'm his friend.' The watchfulness in the boy's face was now quite open.

'Which are you friends with most — your father or your mother?'

'We're all friends.' The face had closed down, though the polite gravity was still undamaged.

'And there's no difference?' she asked, yearning obscurely for the power to make some breach in the child's armour — not to damage him, dear God, but to enter in and feel herself welcomed.

Teddy said nothing. Janet, realising that she was still on her feet, sank down into the chair again. The hostility, the hard, bright alertness, was ebbing away from her, and she was powerless to arrest it; it was almost a physical sensation of loss that she felt — as if, wandering in a desert, she had spilt her only cup of water, and now had to watch it sinking remorselessly into the sand at her feet.

She had enough control left not to bury her face in her hands, as impulse bade; but for a moment she supported her forehead on one hand as if it had become intolerably heavy. And when she looked up, Teddy was standing beside her.

'I'll keep you company, if you like,' he said, 'till my mother comes in. Then you won't mind waiting a bit and we shan't have to take my Dad away from his work.'

'You're sorry for me, aren't you?' she asked.

'Yes,' Teddy said simply. 'You're very sad.'

But this is absurd! a voice cried in Janet's head, shouting so loudly that she jumped, and glanced at Teddy to see if he too had heard it. Absurd! Of course it was. A nice little child-pathos scene out of Victorian melodrama: 'Pitty lady, why is oo so sad?' 'I have sorrows, my dear, whose names you do not know, and whose natures, pray God, you will never learn.' Pah! She stood up again, impatient for action.

'Teddy——'

It was on her tongue to demand, as flatly and insistently as might be necessary, an immediate end to this intolerable half-situation — to compel him, *at once*, to produce his father. The load of grief and anger within her shifted dangerously and threatened to overthrow her altogether. But as she spoke, her eye, traversing the window, was caught by something she saw at the gate.

The sitting-room faced the front garden and the quiet road. Unlatching the gate, holding a shopping-basket in her hand, was Ruth Cowley. It could be no one else; even if the housewifely attitude and the casual movements had not unmistakably shown that this was the mistress of the house, Janet's instinctive reaction told her that this, at last, was her enemy.

She stood motionless, watching. Ruth Cowley turned and latched the gate behind her, then came on up the path. Janet felt every muscle in her body go tense, then slack, then tense again. Anger, weariness and pity, in successive waves, thundered across her being like cavalry over a plain. Here was the woman at last — good! Now to confront her. *And do what?* Never mind what — to tip some of this heavy weight on to her, that was all, that was enough.

Ruth Cowley, serenely unconscious of what confronted her, had by this time walked, with easy step, about a third of the way from the gate to the front door. And suddenly Janet knew that it was no use.

However much of her burden she contrived to throw on to Ruth, would her own share be any the lighter? Would not the past that she still carried take on, at once, an extra weight equal, and more than equal, to the difference?

She turned from the window. 'Teddy,' she said calmly, 'have you got a garden at the back of the house?'

'Yes,' he said: nothing in his face showed surprise, except that his eyes became slightly rounder.

'Will you show me round it?'

He hesitated for a second. 'There's not much growing,' he said. 'We let the soil rest in the winter.'

'But you'll show me, won't you?' she said, smiling. 'I like to see gardens, even when they haven't anything growing in them.'

With no further words, Teddy led the way; they went back into the entrance hall, and Janet fancied as they passed the front door that she could feel the approaching shadow of Ruth Cowley leaning heavily on the opaque glass. Then they were going down a passage and out of the side door.

Was it her imagination, or did she hear the front door click open in the instant that Teddy preceded her out of the house? Probably. Things are seldom as neat as that. With this thought she greeted the open air, feeling like a collier coming up from the darkest and most oppressive gallery.

Teddy made one or two disjointed, polite remarks as they moved down the garden path. Nothing that they saw leapt to the eye at all sharply. Neither of them, for instance, knew that the upturned box beside the toolshed was the one on which the philosopher had

sat during that first conversation with George Links,
a season and three tragedies ago. It was just a wintry,
suspended garden. Janet made no effort to follow
Teddy's mechanically offered discourse. Only the
last words he had spoken in the house circled and
circled in her brain. *We let the soil rest in the winter.*
What else can we do? The soil must rest.

They walked, without stopping, round the frozen
compound that had been green with plants and would,
in some unimaginable time, be so again. The harsh, grey
air brushed at their hair and skin. Janet saw that Teddy
was shivering. Of course, of course, he had only his
indoor clothes on. She ought never to have brought
him out.

'Teddy, go in now,' she said, bending down to him.

'But we've only just come out.'

'It was enough for me to see the garden. Go in now,
dear.'

'And what about you?' he said, standing quite
still.

'I shall go round the side of the house and see myself
out at the front gate.'

'But I thought you wanted . . .'

'No. There's nothing I want, Teddy.'

'You've changed your mind?' he insisted.

'Something like that.'

He went across the lawn, with only one doubtful
glance back at her. Seeing that she was really walking
along the path that led away round the side of the
house, he smiled, as if with sudden relief, and waved
his hand.

'Goodbye,' he called.

'Goodbye, Teddy. Thank you.'

A Travelling Woman

Janet walked quickly to the front of the house and down the path. The click of the garden gate, as she pushed it open, seemed to cancel her visit. Not even a memory remained; the house held nothing that concerned her — two strangers, merely, who had never seen her face.

It was better that way. The time for bitterness was over. She walked on, content to be aware of nothing but the winter and the empty pavement.

THE END

71
72
74
75
76
77
79
83
85